*Also in Fontana*

The 2nd Fontana Book of Great Horror Stories
The 3rd Fontana Book of Great Horror Stories
The 4th Fontana Book of Great Horror Stories
*Ed. Christine Bernard*
The 5th Fontana Book of Great Horror Stories
The 6th Fontana Book of Great Horror Stories
The 7th Fontana Book of Great Horror Stories
The 8th Fontana Book of Great Horror Stories
*Ed. Mary Danby*

The Elemental
*R. Chetwynd-Hayes*
The Valley of Spiders
*H. G. Wells*
Lord Halifax's Ghost Book
Lord Halifax

Sea Tales of Terror
*Ed. J. J. Strating*
Cornish Tales of Terror
*Ed. R. Chetwynd-Hayes*
London Tales of Terror
*Ed. Jacquelyn Visick*
Scottish Tales of Terror
*Ed. Angus Campbell*

The 2nd Fontana Book of Great Ghost Stories
The 4th Fontana Book of Great Ghost Stories
The 5th Fontana Book of Great Ghost Stories
The 6th Fontana Book of Great Ghost Stories
The 8th Fontana Book of Great Ghost Stories
*Ed. Robert Aickman*
The 9th Fontana Book of Great Ghost Stories
*Ed. R. Chetwynd-Hayes*

# Frighteners

*Edited by Mary Danby*

Fontana/Collins

First published by Fontana Books 1974



Made and printed in Great Britain by
William Collins Sons & Co Ltd Glasgow

# CONTENTS

# INTRODUCTION

All too often the horror and/or ghost addict picks up a 'new' book, only to find the same hoary old classics he has read time and time again in other anthologies. Yet all over the world there are writers currently at work on weird, exciting and, above all, *new* horror and ghost stories. Unfortunately, though, few anthologists seem to have time for these authors. They want 'names' on their Contents pages, presumably on the assumption that only a 'name' can produce a well-written, imaginative piece of fiction – or perhaps in the belief that readers (or could it be reviewers?) are not interested in 'unknowns'.

FRIGHTENERS does not contain a single overdone classic. In fact, all seventeen stories appear here in print for the first time. Their authors are all writers who are deservedly making names for themselves in this field, and it may well be that among these stories of today lie tomorrow's classics. If so, I trust that they will avoid the infuriating fate of being 'done to death'.

MARY DANBY

## FOR THE LOVE OF PAMELA

*Kay Leith*

Once, in my weary search for the right place, an estate agent said: 'There's a buyer for every house, no matter how odd.' It was in connection with a remark I had made about one peculiar place that seemed all front – no back nor middle, just front. The agent said: 'One day somebody will walk in and say, "This is for me."'

When Pamela and I first saw 12, Drayfield Grove we felt that, for us, it was that house and no other. Built around the turn of the century, it had a clean stone front and gracious bow windows – a house of character.

I didn't know then, naturally, that I would rue the day I ever clapped eyes on the place.

But *then* it meant that, once the contracts had been exchanged, we could name the day. Everything went without a hitch. Decoratively, it was a bit of a mess, which was why the price was within our range, but we intended to take care of that ourselves.

Pamela and I believed that pleasures deferred are sweeter; therefore we had not anticipated marriage, and didn't mind being labelled old-fashioned.

The first intimation of something sinister came when I was at the house myself one morning, checking electric points and making a rough list of what we needed for each room.

The place seemed to purr like a cat as I wandered from room to room, forming my plans. It was on the half-landing, at the heart, so to speak, of the two-storey house, that something seemed to beckon me.

Without thinking why, I went into the sun-filled room that faced the back garden, looking on to the spears of lilac blooms. It was beautifully proportioned, with a carved, marble-topped fireplace, too fine to rip out. This, I thought, will make a superb sittingroom-cum-workroom for Pamela.

I stood gazing out at the lilacs and, quite distinctly, the floorboards under my feet quivered slightly – so quickly and so briefly that I doubted that it had happened at all. The house was too solidly built to tremble at the passing of heavy traffic.

The front door bell rang. Pamela had brought the makings of the light lunch we'd decided to have there in the house that day. Her eyes, warm hazel, danced in her beautiful face with happiness and conspiracy.

'I bought a bottle of wine!'

'Bang goes a yard of curtain,' I said, pretending dismay. 'It'll be sackcloth instead of brocade, at this rate.'

'Oh, isn't it lovely!' Her long, luxuriant black hair swung gaily as she looked about. Her slim, white fingers caressed the walls.

Just watching her face, as she skipped in and out of the rooms, gave me more pleasure than I'd known for years. She had a tremendous capacity for the enjoyment of simple things.

She doted on the house, thrilled by the promise of the future. I made mental notes of her suggestions. It would be as she wished it to be.

'Gosh, I'm suddenly chilly!' she said, her bare arms goose-pimpled, as we reached the half-landing.

Quickly, she turned to go down for her coat. I was ahead of her on the landing and in no position to catch her when she seemed to trip and went tumbling down the wooden stairs.

'Pam!' I yelled, leaping down two at a time, beside myself with fright.

Dazedly, she looked up at me, hurt disbelief on her face. 'Joe, oh, Joe,' she gasped. 'What happened?'

'Are you hurt?' I ascertained that nothing was broken.

'No, no.' She tried laughing it off, blaming her fashionable shoes, but the incident, oddly enough, made her jittery and uneasy.

She followed me around as though unwilling to let me out of her sight. At three-thirty I suggested that we should stop for the day, but she insisted that, although shaken, she was all right and that I should stay on to finish the measuring-up.

When she had gone, the atmosphere became warmer. It was quite definite and distinct, but I attributed that to my exertions.

The following Saturday, it being Easter, we planned to camp there and work through the weekend and Bank Holiday. Pamela brought along a couple of her brother's sleeping-bags and enough food for our needs.

By Saturday at lunchtime I'd finished stripping the old paper off the walls of the room on the half-landing.

It is difficult – no, impossible – to describe this adequately, but the walls seemed to co-operate in some peculiar way, as though they were shedding the strips of paper like constricting garments.

When I finished and looked around at the results of my labours, it seemed that – lewdly almost, coyly certainly – the room seemed to enjoy being looked at in its nudity of bare plaster.

'You're having hallucinations,' I accused myself wryly, sitting on the floor and lighting a cigarette.

I tried to find something funny in the idea of a sexually aware room. For some reason, which defied analysis, it didn't seem funny at all. My mind switched off; I was attuned to purely sensual things.

There was a barely perceptible throbbing coming from somewhere. It seemed to travel up through the floor and invade my body. Involuntarily, I lay back and closed my eyes.

The reverberations lulled, soothing and exciting at the same time. I was sinking, drifting, succumbing.

'Joe?'

Reluctantly, I opened my eyes, dragging my consciousness back. What now? Why didn't Pam let me lie there, undisturbed?

'Joe? What are you doing?'

The door opened, the throbbing receded, and I felt exposed, as though I'd been caught in some forbidden act. Utterly enervated, I staggered to my feet.

'Lunch is ready,' said Pamela, looking at me curiously.

Vaguely resentful, I balked at any explanation. I wanted only to be alone.

'All right. I'll be down in a minute, when I've finished my cigarette.'

'Don't be long. It's hot.'

Over lunch I managed to shove the experience into the back of my mind. I shied away from examining it.

Before the shops closed finally for two whole days, I dashed out to buy the white spirit I'd forgotten earlier. I left Pamela in the kitchen, washing the paintwork and singing to the music from her transistor.

When I returned half an hour later she was sitting on the stairs, shaking like a leaf and as pale as death.

'Joe!' She wrapped me in a wiry, demanding grip. 'Something spoke to me!'

It was like trying to extricate myself from a coiled spring. 'Take it easy,' I said, putting my arms round her shivering shoulders. 'What spoke to you?'

'I don't know.' She shuddered. 'I was in the kitchen and it seemed to come up behind me.'

I stared my disbelief. 'The house is empty but for us.'

'I know that. Nevertheless, somebody whispered at me.'

'A man?'

'I don't know.' Her eyes were wide, fearful, staring in the direction of the kitchen.

'What did it say?'

'Oh, Joe! It was – it was horrible!' She hid her face in her trembling hands.

I prised her hands away. 'What did the whisper say?'

She looked away, avoiding my eyes. 'Peculiar, weird, disgusting things, Joe.'

Nonplussed, I led her into the lower front room where our camp table and chairs were. 'Look, you've had some sort of delusion. Sit down and I'll go and search the place.'

'Delusion?' She looked up at me indignantly. 'Do you think that I'm imagining things?'

I knelt before her. 'Of course not, but if you were working with your arms over your head, you may have had a blackout. Stay here. I'll go and make sure there's nobody in the house. I'll make a cup of coffee as well.'

She clutched my hand. 'Joe, there's something weird here. Don't leave me.'

'I'm only going around the house. You'll be all right.'

I went along the passage to the kitchen, catlike, examining every shadow. The basin and sponge were as she had left them on the draining board, the place empty. I filled the kettle and plugged it in, leaning against the table.

Just at my right ear, a caressing, breathless voice whispered: 'Darling lover . . .'

My heart and guts turned to cold stone, the blood in my veins congealed to ice. But above all, I felt inexpressibly unclean.

'Come!' the voice urged.

Without having to be told, I knew where it was. In a daze, I left the kitchen.

'Joe?' came Pam's voice.

'All right. Just going to check upstairs.' My tones were normal so as not to cause her alarm . . . but at the same time I didn't want any interference, any diversion from my exciting purpose.

When I opened the door on the half-landing a fetid warmth met me, and the throbbing came up through the soles of my shoes. Invisible hands reached out to me. I tottered forward, one step, two.

The throbbing increased; my ears sang with salacious suggestions. I was drowning in a hot bath of sensation.

Afraid suddenly, I hissed, 'No! Leave me alone!'

The phantom hands loosened, the throbbing eased, the flood receded.

With a great effort of will I closed the door, and stood sweating, shaking, wondering where I'd found the strength to break the spell.

Pamela was standing at the foot of the stairs, gazing up at me, and I knew where my strength to break free had come from. The antithesis of the evil thing that inhabited the house, she, in her goodness, was the best equipped to fight it.

She saw the look on my face, which must have confirmed any conclusions she'd reached herself.

'There's something very odd here,' I admitted when I could speak. 'There's no point in denying it – it's too dangerous to ignore.'

It was fairly obvious to me that, whatever it was, it was antipathetic to – probably jealous of – Pamela.

'Yes – and I don't think it likes me,' she said. 'The other day – on the stairs – I didn't trip. It was as if the stairs disappeared into blackness.'

'Well, what do we do, Pam? I vote that we go home. We don't know how powerful this thing is.'

She shook her head. 'I don't like the idea that we are being driven out by something as evil as that, Joe.'

'Better safe than sorry.'

We argued. I was all for prudence, frankly scared for her safety. Pamela grew more indignant by the minute that anything, mortal or otherwise, should force us to alter our plans and deprive us of the enjoyment of our home.

Over a drink at the local that night, we were still undecided, but away from the house we felt braver. Surrounded by bibulous holiday-makers, it was inconceivable that we could be threatened by anything so ethereal.

'We planned to do so much,' reasoned Pam. 'The entire weekend will be wasted.'

'It's risky.'

'If we stay together all the time, it will be quite safe,' she assured me. 'Then, next week, we can get someone from the psychic phenomena people to examine the place.'

I gave in, unwilling to be less brave than she was. We crawled into our sleeping-bags downstairs at about midnight, a trifle tipsy, certainly quite cheerful. We even called out rude suggestions up the gloomy stairs, collapsing in merriment at our audacity.

I slept only fitfully, forever waking to check, in the light of my torch, that Pamela's dark head still lay on her pillow, and that the shiny cover of her sleeping-bag moved to her gentle breathing.

As dawn broke I fell into a deeper sleep.

Warning bells clanged in my brain. The sun touched my face, and my eyes snapped wide open. What had I been thinking of! It was criminal to have slept! I shot up into a sitting position.

I needn't have whipped myself into such a panic. There she was. Safe enough, lying with her eyes open, smiling at me.

I grinned back.

There was the clink of bottles from a passing milk-float, which made me conscious of my thirst. 'How about some coffee?'

Pamela yawned and stretched her bare arms luxuriously above her head. The sun bathed her satin skin and flowing hair. She looked amazingly refreshed and rested.

I rose, went over, and knelt beside her. She stretched her arms again, and I realized she was nude. Then she lowered her arms, letting them circle down around my neck.

She was pulling me down to her, and I was drowning in a hot, throbbing sensation.

'Darling lover . . .' the filthy thing said out of the purity of Pamela's mouth.

# THE MASK

*Sydney J. Bounds*

'Not another witch!' Jane Clay exclaimed as she opened the front door and peered into the chill October mist. 'It's Roberta . . . I think.'

Jane took her guest's besom and placed it in the hall-stand; that made the third. Even for Hallowe'en, she thought, they might have shown rather more originality. Still, she herself was the only black cat so far . . .

'Grab yourself a drink, dear. Straight through to the kitchen – Wally's running the bar.'

As Jane circulated amongst her guests, the party started to come to life. Music throbbed from the big lounge and she caught snatches of small talk.

'Majorca? We went there last year . . .'

'Remember Margot's party?'

'You know Stan, of course . . .'

Most of her guests knew each other without masks. But tonight, dressed for Hallowe'en, there had been moments of uncertainty, a certain reserve. She glanced at her wrist-watch; too early to serve the meal yet. She edged along a crowded passage echoing with laughter. Pete, in old-fashioned bathing costume and flower-pot hat, was doing his imitation of Farouk again. The kitchen was jammed with men holding glasses and telling jokes.

'Dancing in the lounge,' she announced briskly, 'and some of the girls need partners.'

The kitchen was the only brightly-lit room in the house; elsewhere, candles guttered and smoked, creating shifting shadow-shapes. The music stopped and the doorbell chimed into a silence.

'Wally, can you put on some more records?'

She darted to the door, opened it. A masked face loomed out of the darkness, startling her. 'Oooh . . . yours is the most hideous yet!'

'So glad you don't like it. I went to a lot of trouble, specially to get it for your party.'

'It's you, Len.'

Jane felt a warm glow of pleasure spread through her plump body. She hadn't been sure that Len Roberts of the *Echo* would come at all; a pleasant young man from the local paper – an eligible bachelor, handsome and easy-going, popular with the girls.

'Come on in.'

Len inserted himself into a hall overflowing with people; so many that Jane had invited had actually come it was something of a crush. And not all of them took the Hallowe'en bit seriously. Too many wore fancy dress rescued from other parties.

Len's mask was undoubtedly the *tour de force*; it really frightened.

Jane looked more closely, a delicate shiver trembling along her spine. The waxen skin was drawn tight as a drum, thread-like scars mapped a face of consummate evil, the mouth gaped maniacally.

'Scary,' she murmured. 'Where on earth did you dig that up?'

'It's a death mask,' Len said proudly. 'Guaranteed genuine, I promise.'

'You must –'

A blonde in a plain white dress gave a small, shocked shriek.

'Len, I don't think you know Shirley-Anne.'

'Not yet. But I hope to.'

'I'm the young virgin,' Shirley-Anne said. 'You know, the sacrifice bit.'

'And are you?' Death Mask leered.

Jane left them together. In the lounge, the dishes of crisps and crackers and cheese straws were almost empty. She wriggled her way into the kitchen, clutching her long black tail.

'All right you lot, move along – it's time to dish up. Clear a space on the table, Wally.'

She opened the oven and brought out the chickens. Then, for a time, she was busy handing round plates as her husband carved.

Len had Shirley-Anne pinned in a corner, talking earnestly at her. 'It's real enough. Remember Martin Fletcher? Or perhaps you don't – he might have been before your time . . . Local boy makes bad . . . Had the nasty habit of cutting up young girls and packing their dismembered bodies in trunks.

Till he was caught and hanged. His death mask was made officially . . . I had to pull strings to borrow it tonight.'

'It gives me the shivers. Will you take it off? To please me?'

'Sorry, no can do.' Len's laugh grated harshly; perhaps he'd had a few drinks on the way. 'It's just the job for Hallowe'en.'

By now everyone had a piece of chicken and Jane poured herself a drink and sank into a vacant chair. Parties were so exhausting . . .

She looked round, spotted Shirley-Anne moving into the back room, pursued by Len in his death mask. Quite a catch for her if he were serious. Splinters of conversation drifted Jane's way:

'Any port left, Wally?'

'Did you hear the one about the Scotsman and the Jew – '

Music pumped out of the lounge, seemingly louder, filling the house with pulsing rhythm like the throbbing of a giant heart. Jane pushed to her feet and began circulating again.

Shirley-Anne caught her arm, face white as she whispered: 'Can't you get that ghastly man off my back? He won't take off his mask and it scares me sick, truly it does.'

Jane stifled impatience. 'It's Len Roberts of the *Echo*. You don't want to ditch him, surely?'

'I surely do! He keeps on and on about that dreadful murderer and – '

'It's only a Hallowe'en mask, Shirl. Forget it. Grab yourself a fresh drink.'

The party grew wilder, approaching its climax. Drinks went down faster, the music pulsated louder, laughter became shrill. Someone had borrowed a sheet – not our best, Jane hoped – pretending to be a ghost. Couples paired off in darkening corners as the candles guttered low. The air was hot and smoky.

It must be getting late, she thought vaguely, aware of aching feet. But a successful party; one of her best. She glimpsed Len, still pursuing Shirley-Anne . . . and in the dim light his mask did look horrific. Not funny at all. *Evil.*

'Dance, Jane?'

Somebody had put on a Glenn Miller record. She hitched up her tail, 'Yes, please.' The music recalled old times, made her feel sentimental.

Later, she felt a draught of cold air. The front door stood open and people were beginning to leave. She excused herself and went into the hall.

Wally, stubbing out a cigarette, said casually: 'Drinks are about finished.'

She glanced at her watch; one-thirty. 'I'll just make some coffee before they go.'

She squeezed along the passage to the kitchen. The door was shut. She moved the handle but the door didn't open. Surprised, she called: 'Wally, have you locked the kitchen?'

'Of course not.'

Her husband tried the door. It wouldn't budge. Above the music, she thought she heard a muffled voice from the kitchen and called out: 'Open up in there!'

Pete guffawed. 'Only a petting session, Jane. Not to worry. Forget the coffee.'

Jane made a small frown, 'It's annoying, though.'

Someone else was leaving. 'Nice party, Jane. You must come to ours.' Outside, cars revved up and headlights speared the darkness.

Wally, handing round hats and coats, said: 'It must be Len and Shirley-Anne. In the kitchen, I mean. I can't see who else is missing.'

Odd, Jane thought, considering how she'd been trying to lose him all evening. But Len without his death mask was a different proposition; a real charmer.

The music stopped and, in the silence, a wheezing sounded from behind the kitchen door. It had a desperate quality.

Pete pointed at the floor. 'What's that?'

Something wet and sticky oozed from under the door.

'Wally!' Jane's voice sharpened. 'Get a screwdriver – force it open.'

The laboured wheezing went on and on, a frightening sound. Wally came back with a large screwdriver, jammed the blade into the crack between the door and the frame, and levered with it. There was a splintering noise and the door sprang open.

Jane looked in and saw Len Roberts struggling violently with the mask, his body jack-knifed and his hands shaking. She saw her favourite carving knife and knew she would never be able to use it again. She turned away, gagging on vomit.

From a distance, she heard Len's voice: 'I can't get it off . . . for God's sake, *help me*! The mask . . . I . . . can't . . . get . . . it . . . off . . .'

# OLD HETHER'S PICTURE

*Joyce Marsh*

Ted Williams wielded his spade with the consummate ease of long practice; the clean, sharp blade whistled down, slicing into the heavy clay soil. He straightened for a moment and looked back with satisfaction at the long narrow strip of newly-dug soil. Almost at his feet a fat robin joyfully gorged himself on the minute insects revealed by Ted's efforts.

Suddenly, out of the corner of his eye, Ted glimpsed a twitch of the curtains in the window of the cottage behind him. He made no sign that he had seen the movement, but with a wry smile returned instantly to his work. Mrs Hetherington, or 'Old Hether' as he privately called her, had begun the curious game that she played every week when he came to tend her garden.

The old woman was an enigma. She had lived in the cottage for only a little over a year, but no one knew whence she came or what eccentric whim had led her, in old age, to leave familiar surroundings and settle amongst strangers in this remote little village. Indeed, as far as Ted knew, he was the only person who had ever seen her face to face or spoken to her. Her simple, basic needs were ordered from the general store by means of curt notes apparently delivered by hand at dead of night.

Ted had obtained his employment with her merely because he had tended the garden for the previous occupants and had continued to do so in the hope (subsequently justified) that she would accept and pay for his services. At first she had been the object of much curiosity and speculation in the village, but, in the absence of any further information about her, interest had waned and she was left in peace to pursue the life of a complete recluse.

In the first few weeks of his acquaintance with Old Hether, Ted had never caught more than a shadowy glimpse of his employer, until one morning she had begun the curious procedure that was to set the pattern for their future relationship. She watched him at his work, furtively peering from behind the curtains of first one window and then another until, as he neared the end of his work, she would open the door a fraction and stand in the dark shadows of the hall. Then, timing the movement to coincide with the completion of the job in hand, she would rattle the little bunch of keys which always dangled from her wrist. Ted had soon learnt that this was intended as a signal that he could leave his work and go into the cottage. The old woman had always kept out of sight as he passed through the dark hall and into the kitchen where a thick earthenware mug of tea and his wages lay waiting on the kitchen table. At first this curious routine had puzzled and irritated him, but with the instinctive, kindly tolerance of the eccentricities of old age he had finally accepted her way and drunk his tea, pocketed his money and left without even as much as a glimpse of the old lady.

This routine had continued unchanged for some weeks until one morning, about four or five months before, he had suddenly heard the faint rustle of her skirts and had realized that she was watching him from the shadowy hallway outside the kitchen door. Unwilling to annoy or embarrass her, he had given no indication that he knew she was there, but had continued quietly sipping his tea. At last, no doubt encouraged by his voluntary adherence to her curious rules of procedure, she had stepped boldly into the kitchen and joined him at the table, sipping her tea from a tiny, ornately-decorated cup.

For a while they had drunk their tea in silence, her pale, watery old eyes never leaving his face while he waited patiently for her to speak, and when she eventually did so her voice was hoarse and croaking, as if stiffened by long disuse.

She had about her an air of almost maidenly diffidence which ill-suited an old woman of such immense stature, for everything about her was large from her bony, hooked nose to her great feet, only just visible beneath the voluminous skirts of her old-fashioned dress. Her thick, muscular arms and still ample bosom strained relentlessly against the thin black silk of her bodice.

Since that first occasion she had always joined him while he drank his tea, and over the months a kind of relationship had developed between Old Hether and her jobbing gardener. Yet, even now, he knew no more about her than he had on the first day he had seen her. For never in any of their talks had she given the slightest hint or dropped a casual word about herself or her past life. It was almost as if she had sprung to life already in old age without home, family or connections. She knew a great deal about him, however, since her entire conversation consisted of questions, probing and seeking into the tiniest detail of his life.

She knew about the devastating mental collapse that had robbed his wife of her reason and left her a pathetic simpleton. She knew too of the desperate struggles he endured to earn a living for his family as an odd job man because he must never go more than a few minutes' walk away from his helpless wife.

If the truth were known, Ted did not much enjoy these sessions, as her questions brought to the surface sorrows and regrets which were better left to lie, half-forgotten, beneath the surface of his mind. Time and again he had resolved to answer her no more, but each time, under the strange compulsion of her pale eyes and the hooked nose hovering over the rim of her cup, he had felt his resolution waver and fade away. Besides, she was kind enough in her own way, his wages had been increased and more than once a trifling gift for his wife or the children had been left by the mug of tea. So with a kind of rough philosophy he was prepared to endure her whims if it gave her pleasure and did him no harm.

The summer sun was hot and the long flower-bed seemed interminable. Fortunately he was nearing the end and could soon enjoy his tea and a brief rest in the cool kitchen. With a deft twist of the wrists he turned over the last spit and on the instant his ear, cocked for the sound, caught the slight jangle of her keys. Pausing only to lean his spade against the fence he went straight into the cottage.

As he entered the kitchen he saw at once that the routine had changed, for she was already there waiting for him. But there was no sign of his tea. She nodded and gave one of her rare smiles.

'Do you mend things?'

'Depends,' he answered laconically, whereupon she led the way out of the kitchen and back down the hall. She unlocked the door of her parlour and together they went in.

The room was in fact quite sparsely furnished, but since each piece was far too large for its surroundings it appeared to be unbelievably cluttered, an impression by no means lessened by the overwhelming dominance of a large picture hanging on the chimney breast. There was no need for her to indicate the job she had in mind, since the solitary armchair stood leaning over at a drunken angle. A brief glance showed Ted that it was a simple matter to repair it, and since he was often required to do such work he had all the tools he needed in his wooden hand-cart.

As he worked she watched him in silence from the doorway, but he was less aware of her than he was of the dark, brooding picture on the wall behind him. There was a certain familiarity about it which he could not explain, and as soon as he had finished the work he turned to examine the picture more closely.

'Do you like my picture?'

He did not answer her for a moment. He was still trying to remember where he had seen it before.

'Seems to me I've seen it somewhere before.'

For the first time ever, he heard her give a hoarse, grating chuckle.

'Not that one, you haven't. That's my picture and there ain't another one the same anywhere, not anywhere.'

'Well, I've seen summat like it.'

'Like it! Ah yes, like it, but not the same. You've mebbe seen a picture called "The Cornfield" done by some painter named Constable.'

Her words instantly explained the picture's air of familiarity, for he had a print of that picture at home. In happier days his wife had collected the tops of soap-powder packets to obtain it as a free gift, but Old Hether was right – the two pictures were not quite the same. He was about to ask her where the difference lay, but her unmistakable pride in the uniqueness of her possession had loosened her tongue.

'My picture was done first, though. It was painted by a young chap who was learning 'is business from this Constable, but he was no good at it, poor lad, and he knew it. They say he done this picture as 'is last try and it were no good so he hung himself. Then Constable painted the picture again only he didn't draw in the house 'cos that's where the young chap lived and where he done himself in.'

Ted looked again at the painting and wondered why he had needed anyone to point out the difference, for now it was plain to see. In the foreground, where in Constable's famous painting a small boy sprawled on the grass beside a pool, in this picture that whole corner was occupied by a squat, ugly little house.

He understood, too, why Constable's tragic pupil had so despaired of his talent, for his brush had been unable to impart the tiniest hint of beauty or life to the dismal cottage. Although the cornfield in the background and the trees on the right were bright and sunlit, no touch of light or shade relieved the drab ugliness of the little house. It brooded over the whole painting with a sort of grim foreboding, as if it only waited for the tragedy that was about to take place within its walls.

Ted shrugged off the morbid fancy inspired by the dismal picture and its tragic history. Then another thought occurred to him. It was an original painting, an old one at that, and even if the artist had not been a pupil of Constable at least parts of the picture bore a strong resemblance to Constable's masterpiece. It might, therefore, be valuable.

'Is it worth anything?'

It was obvious that her expansive mood had evaporated as she answered with her accustomed brevity.

'I was offered five hundred pounds once.'

He turned to the picture again, this time with renewed respect, but Old Hether was not apparently inclined to indulge his further curiosity, for with a brusque, 'Come on then if you've finished,' she led the way out of the parlour and back into the kitchen where, over tea, they resumed the customary pattern of their one-sided conversations.

Some weeks had passed since the incident of the broken chair and autumn had fallen upon Old Hether's garden.

Dry, russet leaves, more beautiful in death even than they had been in the lush green of their beginnings, had descended in clouds, clogging drains, pathways and borders. Diligently Ted raked, swept and hoarded them into great glowing, golden piles, but the glorious beauty around him only served to depress his spirits, for autumn had heralded the onslaught of winter's deathly chill and there were few in the village willing to pay a jobbing gardener to watch helplessly over barren, icy soil.

With a final flick of the broom he pushed the last leaves together and stood for a moment watching the thin plume of sweet-smelling smoke curl upwards. His ear was cocked for the rattle of Old Hether's keys. It did not come. Not once during the morning had he glimpsed a twitching curtain and now, though the job was finished, the door remained firmly closed.

He frowned in puzzlement, but it took only a moment for him to arrive at his decision and, for the first time without her signalled invitation, he opened the door and went into the cottage.

It was very quiet inside as he went first into the kitchen, but she was not there. Her old-fashioned open range was quite cold and the tea things stood undisturbed on the shelf. He called softly. There was no answer, so he walked back down the hall and tried the parlour door. It was unlocked, and there inside he found her.

She was lying on her back on the floor near the chair. Her eyes were closed and her face had a terrible bluish tinge with the dark lips drawn back in a grimace of pain. Ted flung himself down on his knees beside her, but even before he touched her ice-cold hands and listened in vain for a heartbeat he knew that she was dead.

He leapt to his feet, gazing wildly around the room as if some advice or assistance could be found lurking in its quiet corners – and perhaps it could, for the calm, unruffled quiet washed away the shock of finding her so. He looked down at her in pity. He was sorry that she was dead and he softly touched her face as if trying to smooth away that twisted grimace.

Gradually, pity for her gave way to self-interest. She had had a long life and now it was over. She was gone, but with her passing he had lost a job – and she was one of the few who had promised him work throughout the coming winter.

His eyes left her face and almost at once fell upon the picture on the chimney breast.

'Five hundred pounds.'

The words clicked slowly through his brain. With five hundred pounds he could laugh at winter – all his winters. He could send his wife to one of those homes where she might find some measure of happiness amongst others of her own kind, whilst he could go back to earning real money again in the factory.

The picture might have been his, for he was Old Hether's only friend and if she had died slowly she might have said, 'I want you to have the picture when I'm gone.' Yes, she might quite easily have said that if she had thought of it. After all, who else was there to claim her things? Probably they would seek out some distant relative who had barely heard of the old girl and certainly had not cared about her. People like that had no right to the picture – at least, they had less right to it than the man who had befriended the lonely old woman.

In his imagination it was almost as if he had heard her speak the words, and his thoughts ran on; there might be other things she would have wanted him to have. All her possessions were old and he was worldly enough to know that age increases value.

He looked slowly around the room. A tiny china shepherdess smiled down at him from her shelf. He lifted her down, his rough fingers caressing the delicate porcelain, and placed her carefully on the floor near the door. She was soon joined by a silver dish and a heavy glass bowl. He would not take everything – they would expect her to have some trinkets left. Besides, he only wanted what might rightfully have been his – the sort of things she might have left him.

All the other rooms were locked and he shuddered as he took the keys from her wrist, but he went on through the cottage, adding to his little collection in the parlour. Finally he turned back to the picture. It was firmly fixed to the wall with strong wire twisted round and round the hook, but at last he had it free and he carefully lifted it down, supporting its weight against his body.

'Hell waits for those who rob the dead.'

The words ran through his mind, but they hung in the atmosphere as if they had been spoken aloud. In the deathly silence of the room there came a tiny sound from behind him, and he spun round, almost falling with the heavy picture clasped across his chest.

She was staring up at him. Her eyes, wide open now, were darker and shone more brilliantly than he had ever seen them and there was a look in them that sent a cold shudder to the very depths of his soul. Her mouth moved silently and soft gurgling noises came from her throat. He had been mistaken, then. A tiny spark of life still burned within her and she had been lying there watching him – watching him take down the picture.

'I wasn't robbing you! You would have given me the picture. It's for the kids. You would have given it to me!' he screamed at her, but the expression in her eyes did not soften as, with a visible effort, she rolled her head from side to side in an unmistakable gesture of negation. Almost with her dying breath she was silently denying him the right to take the picture.

Suddenly her features contorted with pain, and when the spasm died away she clearly and distinctly mouthed the word 'Medicine', and for the first time her eyes left his face. He followed her glance and saw, under the chair, a small bottle of tablets. The top had come off and half the contents were scattered about on the carpet.

Urgently, he put down the picture and, kneeling down, reached across her for the bottle. Her breath was gurgling in her throat and with her face so close to his he could see the light draining from her eyes. She was nearly gone.

But what if the tablets revived her? Supposing she recovered enough to tell of what she had seen? He would be disgraced, pointed at, cursed for a man who robbed the dead.

His fingers curled round the bottle and he sat back on his heels looking down at her. She was so old, so very old, and close to death. Was it fair that he should face disgrace and see his family starve just to give her a few more weeks – days even? She was gasping agonizingly and staring fixedly at the bottle in his hand.

Slowly he stood up and turned round, still holding the tablets. There was a terrible numbing chill spreading through his body as he stood there with bowed head and listened to her die.

Her last breaths left her in high-pitched, whistling gasps, each one farther away from the last. A terrible rattling sound filled the room. It came three times and then – silence.

For a long time he stood there before he dared to look at her.

There was no mistake now. She was dead. Her eyes, wide open, were glazed and dark. He paused to press heavy fingers on the lids to shut them for ever and then, with trembling hands, packed the picture and the other things into his wooden hand-cart and left.

Old Hether's death caused only the merest breath of interest in the village. A few cursory inquiries satisfied the authorities, and on the last, glorious day of a short Indian summer they laid her to rest.

Only Ted, shivering despite the hot sun, stood by her graveside to bid her a last farewell.

He had been right in his supposition; someone, somewhere, discovered relatives with a right to claim her belongings. A few weeks after the funeral they came in two big, shining cars. From his vantage point behind a hedge, Ted heard them squealing and laughing as they romped through her quiet rooms, and he watched them noisily running in and out as they loaded the cars with the spoils of their undeserved inheritance. One of the men caught sight of Ted and called out to him. His voice sounded friendly enough, but with fear and guilt rising to a panic within him, Ted could only stare wildly and run away. As he fled over the fields he prayed that he might never see Old Hether's cottage again, and his prayers were answered, for within a few days the bulldozers had torn it apart and a hundred years of hopes, dreams, laughter and tears lay crushed into a pile of filthy rubbish.

But now Ted was safe – safe to enjoy what he persistently told himself was his rightful inheritance. Secretly, with instinctive cunning, he made several trips into the nearby town to sell the trinkets and bric-a-brac one or two at a time. The antique shops seemed eager to buy and none questioned his right of possession.

When all the small ornaments were gone, he counted his hoard. It came to nearly eighty-one pounds – a small fortune. It meant a warm, well-fed winter for his kids, and she would not begrudge him that.

His arms rested on the table before him, the fingers loosely clasped, encircling his money. His head drooped lower. Somewhere behind him his wife had begun the little whimpering noises which would eventually rise to screaming hysteria. Bitterly he remembered another time and another place when, with bowed head, he had listened to another woman making fearful animal noises, and the chill that had descended on him then was with him still.

Suddenly he shook his head. It was useless to brood on the past. What was done was done, and the picture was his now. Five hundred pounds! It meant comfort, security – perhaps even a little happiness for his wife. That was a great deal to set against just a few more days of life for an old woman.

Now he must consider ways of disposing of the picture. He had been clever over the trinkets – he must be even more clever about selling the picture. He could not take it to the local shops in the town. None of them would offer five hundred pounds – besides, no breath of rumour must seep back to the village. London was the answer, London with its teeming, anonymous millions amongst whom he could pass in secret. There were plenty of Art Galleries and dealers, one of whom might offer him even more than five hundred pounds, and the first thing he would buy was a headstone for Old Hether – she would like that.

For a moment he felt a warm, cosy glow of satisfaction and he leaned back, gazing upwards as if his glance could penetrate the ceiling to see through to the tiny attic room where the picture lay, still wrapped in his old sacking apron.

Since the day he had carried it from Old Hether's cottage he had not dared to look at the picture, but now, suddenly everything was different. He had quieted his conscience with the promise of a headstone. A more cynical man might have realized that this apparent lifting of the burden of guilt was most likely due to a mounting confidence in his safety from detection.

With his children at school the cottage was very quiet except for the soft whimpering of his wife, and he knew that she would remain thus in her corner for a long time. On an impulse he got up and went upstairs.

The attic room was little more than a cupboard tucked under the steep angle of the roof, and he had to bend almost double to creep through the low door. The picture was hidden behind a heap of indescribable rubbish and he had to tread warily, for in places the floor was so rotten that it could collapse under his weight. But the danger in here had made it an ideal hiding place, since the children had long ago been forbidden to enter the attic.

He squatted in front of the picture and slowly, almost reverently, rolled back the sacking. What harm he imagined might have befallen the painting it is hard to know, but he gave a small sigh of relief when he saw that it was safe and sound. He examined the fine detail of the trees and admired the joyful sunlight flowing over the field of ripe corn, then, inevitably, his eye was drawn to the little house. In the dim light of the attic it seemed larger and darker, its dismal, brooding influence dominating the whole painting and robbing it of whatever beauty and light the artist had managed to impart with his sunny background.

Ted bent forward to peer more closely, for his eye, accustomed now to the dim light, had detected a tiny detail hitherto unnoticed. He dragged the heavy picture a few feet until the pale sunshine slanting through the skylight shone directly upon it. Now it was clear and he wondered why he had not seen it before: the door of the house had not been painted shut as he had first thought – it was open a tiny crack, and somehow the artist had conveyed an indefinable disturbance of the atmosphere which suggested that someone, although unseen, was standing behind the partly open door.

Ted stared until his eyes smarted under the concentrated effort, but he could not detect a single line to show where the figure stood, neither could he determine what trick of brush and paint the artist had employed to convey so clearly that someone stood there in the shadows behind the door.

The pale sun was suddenly extinguished by a passing cloud and the light in the attic grew dimmer, too dim to examine the details of the picture any further. With a faint shrug, Ted replaced the sacking over the painting. Downstairs he could hear that his wife was approaching the hysterical climax of her spasm. Hastily he restored his treasure to its hiding place and hurried down to restrain her.

By next morning he had determined that it was safe to dispose of the picture and he planned to take it to London that very day. To avoid being seen in the village wearing his good suit and carrying a large package, he decided to walk to the railway station in the next town with the picture hidden in his hand-cart. He was naïvely proud of his cunning, for pushing the barrow, and with his suit covered by an old coat, no one would guess that he was on any other errand than his usual working day. The only part of his plan that brought a tinge of anxiety was the need to tether his wife like an animal to her bed, but it was for her own protection and, with luck, it might only be for half a day.

These simple arrangements necessitated a very early start and it was barely light as he crept up to the attic to wrap the picture for its journey. So early in the morning was it that his wife and the children were still sleeping and it was very quiet in the cottage. The attic room was cold as the chill winds of early winter blew in through the broken roof.

Carefully he placed an oil lamp on a box in the middle of the floor and dragged the picture in its heavy, ornate frame into the pool of light. For a long moment he stared down at it. He felt an odd reluctance to look at it again, but he could not take it to a dealer shrouded in a piece of dirty sacking – it had to be properly wrapped. With a swift movement he threw back the sacking. At once his eye was drawn to the front door of the house, and what he saw laid a terrible chill upon him, as if an icy hand had clutched at his heart.

With trembling hands he seized the lamp and held it close, peering intently, praying that he had been deceived by a trick of the light. The lamp cast a bright glow and there was no mistake; the door of the painted house stood almost half open now, and in the dark shadows behind he could plainly see the outline of a figure. That figure which he had been unable to discern the day before now stood clearly visible.

It was a woman in long, dark clothing. One hand gripped the edge of the door, but the other reached out through the opening. The sleeve had fallen back and the white arm stretched towards him with one long finger crooked as if beckoning.

The flame in the lamp flickered in the draught and the wavering light rippled over the painting, touching the long, evil finger and making it appear to move and urge him forward, drawing him in towards the half-open door in the painted house.

With an animal-like whimper of fear, Ted threw back the sacking and fled. He dared not now go to London with his picture, so all day long he remained indoors, always conscious of the fearful picture upstairs hanging like a terrible doom over his head. By nightfall, however, his fears had begun to fade. Five hundred pounds were not to be lightly cast away because of his guilt-inspired fancies. The next day the painting must go to London.

But the next day he was plunged again into a different kind of fear. The post brought a letter from a solicitor acting on behalf of Old Hether's relatives. They had missed the picture and inquiries were being made as to its whereabouts. Ted was not, as yet, suspected, but as the only person known to have entered the old woman's cottage he was the first contact in the solicitor's inquiries. He had to accept that it was too risky now to dispose of the picture.

For most of the day the unhappy man tried to busy himself in his garden, but at last, when the house was quiet, he surrendered to the compulsion to look at the picture once more.

The attic was even colder and the lamp that he had forgotten the day before still burned, casting an eerie glow on the shrouded painting. There was a certain courage in the bold gesture with which he threw back the covering, half expecting, half knowing what he would see.

The figure had left the concealing shadows of the doorway and now stood boldly on the front step. A streak of paint sent a shaft of light across her skirt and lit up the bare white arm, but her face was still mercifully dark with shadows. For a long time he squatted in front of the picture. He had the curious notion that if he saw her move he could stop her, but at last his lamp died out and it was still just a picture, dead, unmoving.

Long into the night the picture haunted him. He knew now that he must abandon all thoughts of selling it. Reluctantly he surrendered the hopes and dreams that five hundred pounds might have made reality – but he dared not keep it either. Only one alternative remained.

His tiny backyard was safe from prying eyes as he laid wood, paper and dried garden refuse to build a bonfire. When all was ready he went slowly upstairs to the attic. Firmly he grasped the frame, holding the sacking tightly over the picture. Not even one more look should remain in his memory to torment him. The fire was waiting, there were none to spy upon him, and yet he hesitated. One tiny hope of gain still lurked in his mind. The frame. Who could identify a frame? Ornately carved and gilded as it was it might be worth something. He took out his clasp-knife and threw aside the sacking.

The figure was more than half-way down the garden path. She was no longer beckoning. Her hands lifted her trailing skirts clear of the ground and every line of her body denoted a purposeful stride. She was an extraordinarily large woman, tall and thin, but a shawl covered her head and cast deep, concealing shadows over her face.

With trembling hands Ted pressed the knife to the edge of the painting, but an icy weakness robbed him of the strength to cut the picture from its frame. He flung the knife away and stumbled from the attic, knowing in his heart that he would never be free of his inheritance from Old Hether.

It took the woman in the picture several days to reach the garden gate, and each day she grew larger, blotting out more and more of the picture. Insistently, Ted told himself that he would never look again – he even considered boarding up the attic door to seal off his nightmare for ever – but just as he had been unable to resist Old Hether's insidious questioning, now he could not resist the terrible compulsion of her picture, and each new day saw him creeping into the attic.

Barely a week had passed since he had first seen the figure in the picture and yet in that short time he had grown thin, pale and gaunt-eyed. At first he had spent long hours and sleepless nights sweating and trembling in terror, but on this last morning, with the first flakes of early snow softly kissing the window panes, he crept upstairs with a certain serene resignation.

In his heart he knew that this would be the last time he would need to look at the picture, for the day before the figure had stood at the gate with her hand resting on the latch. She was about to open it, and when she did the last flimsy bastion between himself and his doom would be gone.

The attic was very dark, but the lamp stood ready and he lit it carefully, keeping his back to the picture on the floor. His hand reached for the covering and perhaps a tiny ray of hope still lingered, for he closed his eyes and sent forth a silent prayer for release.

The icy sacking crackled slightly as he turned it aside, and then he was staring down into the cold, wrinkled face of Old Hether. In his heart he had always known that it was her face hidden by the concealing shadows of her shawl, yet now, when the shawl lay across her shoulders, he was ill-prepared for the shock of gazing once more on those features that had so long haunted his dreams.

She had reached the front of the canvas and only the upper half of her body was visible, but one hand was raised with the long, bony fingers held out towards him. Her head and that one hand almost filled the frame, blotting out everything else.

'Leave me be! I meant you no harm. It were for the kids I done it, not for meself. For God's sake leave me be!'

His voice rose to a terrible scream, but the painted eyes neither moved nor flickered. Their implacable hatred was caught on the canvas for ever. He put out a trembling hand, as if to push away those dreadful bony fingers pointing at him, and as he did so he felt his own fingers gripped as if in an icy vice. Desperately he struggled to get free as he felt himself being drawn in slowly, inexorably, towards those still, dead eyes.

His frantic screams flung out on the crisp morning air and brought bewildered friends and neighbours hurrying to his aid. But he was dead when they found him, stretched out on the floor with one hand reaching out to touch an old painting. They huddled in frightened silence in the attic doorway, for there was such terror in his staring eyes and distorted features that none dared enter to close his eyes. Later, even the ambulance attendants, accustomed to violent death and mutilation, shuddered and turned away as they hastily covered his face.

It was not very long before the picture was identified and everyone knew that Ted had stolen it. But why? It was just a worthless old painting, only a poor copy of Constable's 'Cornfield', except that the artist had added a dismal little house with an open door and two figures on the garden path walking towards it. One, a large woman, was leading the other – a man who seemed very reluctant to go in through the door.

# CERA

*Bernard Taylor*

*Ah, yes. Now the fire is taking hold, the flames are growing stronger. The sound of the ocean is quite drowned. When the flames are high enough and fierce enough I shall call the fire brigade. But not yet. Not till the fire's completely out of control. I can't take the chance of the firemen finding . . . anything . . .*

*It's a shame about the beautiful house. Still, it matters little now. They won't be needing it any more. I wonder whether Greg ever did . . .*

Greg Marchant and I grew up in the same little seaside town.

And although we lived right next door to each other we never really became close friends. It was only later, after we had separated and gone our own ways, that our lives became inextricably involved with each other's. But while we were there, growing up to manhood side by side, we were apart. What was established between us was a quiet, reserved friendliness, one that was acknowledged, as it were, from the other side of a room.

One factor – and perhaps the main one – that inhibited any close relationship was the great difference in our respective heights. When fully grown I stood a solid six-foot-four in my bare feet, and Greg an unfortunate five-foot-one. I am sure that, for him as much as for me, the mere mental picture of us side by side was enough to stop us even from walking down the street together. The only times we ever felt at ease in each other's company, as I recall, were the few occasions we happened to meet down on the beach where we swam. There, in the water, the disparity in our sizes didn't matter. Greg seemed more relaxed somehow, gaining a confidence which, on his own two feet, he seemed to lack.

He was a strange-looking young man – even without his lack of stature. With his large, fleshy lips and small teeth, his ears flat to his head, he looked most unprepossessing. Once, when I remarked on his odd looks, and how different was his appearance from that of his parents, I was told by my mother that Greg had been adopted by the Marchants when he was just a baby. Where he had actually come from she did not know. Anyway, Greg was always there, quietly in the background. Until I left home to work in London – then he faded completely. And it was soon after that that I met Cera and fell so hopelessly in love with her.

Our meeting was, in a way, like some awful Hollywood film cliché. Whilst walking down Regent Street one spring afternoon she cannoned straight into me, catching me such a hefty clout on the cheekbone with her forehead that I was momentarily thrown off balance. We clutched each other for a second, like dancers caught in the midst of a step, then, recovering her balance and her dignity, she gave her apologies. There was some grit in her eye, she explained, blinking frantically, the tears streaming down her face. Of course, it was a heaven-sent opportunity for me and I lost no time in demonstrating my prowess with the corner of a handkerchief. Her eyes were dark and round, rather small but enigmatic and quite captivating. I removed the offending foreign body and, with my handkerchief, she dried her tears.

In her hand I noticed that she held a pair of sun-glasses.

'I had just taken them off to polish the lenses,' she said. 'Obviously I chose the wrong moment.'

She had a slight accent. It was almost as if her words were too carefully, too perfectly formed. I have the feeling that she was Italian – perhaps she told me so – I can't remember.

I *can* remember how beautiful she was, though. Very beautiful. And tall. Almost as tall as I. Some men avoid very tall women – understandable in many cases – but I'm sure they wouldn't have avoided Cera . . . Cera . . .

'It's a beautiful name,' I told her. 'It suits you.' I spoke like some lovesick teenager. When she told me her last name I reacted with surprise. It was even more unusual.

'Tiidae?' I said. 'What kind of a name is that?'

She laughed in reply.

'Don't you like it? What can I do about it?'

'You could change it,' I said, laughing in return. 'To Robertson, for instance.'

'Your name wouldn't happen to be Robertson, would it?' she said.

I nodded gravely. 'You really are very astute!'

I made up my mind then that I wanted to marry her. I think I might have been successful had not Greg Marchant come once more upon the scene.

Desperately in love, I invited her to spend the weekend at my parents' house by the sea. A village barbecue had been planned on the beach and I intended to make use of the festive atmosphere to help me in my proposal.

Everything was going well. With the villagers we sat around the fire on that warm, summer night, while the waves of the sea lapped gently just yards away. With the fading of the day Cera had taken off her dark glasses and now her bright eyes shone in the moonlight. She smiled at me, her lovely face framed by her thick, dark hair. I was deliriously happy. I watched her as she rose to her feet, standing above me tall and statuesque like a goddess of ancient times.

'I think, Carl, I would like to swim,' she said, looking down at me. 'Will you come?'

'In a moment,' I said. I wanted, for a while, the sheer

pleasure of watching her from a distance; to bask in my proprietary glow.

She slipped the robe from her shoulders and stood there wearing a most becoming one-piece bathing suit. I could sense the eyes of the villagers turned towards her. Quite unaware, she smiled down at me. 'Don't be long, then.' With the words, she turned to move away.

She stopped so suddenly a moment later, that I looked at once to see what or who had attracted her attention.

It was Greg Marchant.

Rather amused at first, I looked from one to the other as they stood there some feet apart in the glow of the fire. Then I looked at Greg's face more closely. I'll never forget the look in his eyes as he gazed up at her from his lower vantage point. Yes! I remember thinking, you might well look at her so adoringly! But there's no chance for you, I'm afraid, my little friend!

When he came closer I got to my feet and made the necessary introductions. I fully expected that Cera would then make some polite excuse and continue to the water for her swim. But no, she stood there still, and suddenly, quite astounded, I saw the expression in her own dark brown eyes. Where I had expected to see amusement, tolerance, perhaps, I saw instead the reflection of his own adoration! They stood there gazing at each other, rapt, as if no one else existed for them.

It was my imagination, I told myself. Such a thing couldn't possibly be true! How could Greg Marchant, a mere five-foot-one, dream of ever making a match with Cera, who stood at least a foot taller? The idea was ludicrous! It was! Quite ludicrous . . .

But when I returned to London I came alone.

Two weeks later, still solitary in my flat, I read the newspaper clipping sent from home that told of the wedding of Mr Gregory Marchant and Miss Cera Tiidae. There was a photograph, too. The top of his head came just to her shoulder.

'It's grotesque!' I said aloud. 'It can never work. The whole thing is just too silly.'

The smiles in the photograph were happy and I thought at once of their smiles and their laughter when I had watched them from the beach on the night of the barbecue. They had swum together, their bodies flashing, glinting in the moon-sparked water, their laughter bouncing back, echoing to the shore. I had felt embarrassed, but determined not to show it, the smile on my face growing more stiff and wooden with every second.

'Don't hate me, Carl,' Cera had pleaded an hour before I had left for my London train. 'I love him,' she had told me. 'Please try to understand.'

*'Understand!'* I had almost shouted the word back at her. How could she ask me to understand? How could she *expect* me to? She had known Greg for only *two days*! And in that time had thrown aside all that I had offered her. I would never understand, I told myself. Never. How could she do it to me? How? I was twenty-four years old and certain that I would never recover. I hated her then. I hated both of them. Desperately. Had she perhaps given me up for someone who was, at least physically, something of a challenge, it might have been easier to bear. But to lose out to someone who came to just above my elbow was a fact I couldn't bear to think about.

But I *did* think about it. I couldn't stop thinking about it. The thought of Cera and Greg preyed on my mind till I was obsessed with them. I still couldn't believe that I had lost her. It was impossible, I kept telling myself. And yet, there it was. There, too, was the newspaper-clipping, the photograph, and the letter that had more recently arrived from Cera herself. In it she begged me once again to forgive and to try to understand. She was, she said, unbelievably happy. Greg was as well. And all their happiness, all their contentment, they owed to me. It was true; they did.

But they had destroyed *my* happiness, I thought. My own life was shattered. Well, in time they would pay. I was determined.

*Another window in the lounge has just fallen out. Shivered in pieces. The heat must be building up in there. Still, it's not too hot to prevent my getting a quick look into the room. I can just make out the enormous shape there, smoke engulfed, lying on the carpet . . .*

I thought so much about Cera and Greg that when, at last, we actually met – by chance – it came as no great surprise. I knew we would meet again some time, somewhere.

On this occasion I was wandering aimlessly around the Natural History Museum in South Kensington. I had arrived there from the school nearby where I taught English and biology; having an engagement in the West End with a friend, it hardly seemed worth while going home to my flat in Wimbledon, so the museum was as good a place as any in which to kill an hour. The time was just after four-thirty. I had been amusing myself by gazing at a model of an angler fish. Quite inexplicably I had at once been reminded of Cera and Greg. The very size of the female compared with the male was enough to bring the pair at once into my thoughts again. I made my way to the cafeteria, bought a cup of coffee and a sandwich, and sat down. And then I saw them, Greg and Cera, sitting at the table next to mine. It was some moments before either of them saw me and I had, in those moments, ample opportunity to study them.

It must have been over five years since we had last met, I reckoned, and I only hoped that *I* had not changed quite so drastically in that time.

To be absolutely honest, I had never seen a more odd-looking couple in my entire life. Cera, I was sure, had grown larger than ever, while Greg, on the other hand, appeared to have shrunk. And it wasn't only in height that they had changed. They were different in bulk, also. Greg, moving past Cera to hand her a cup of tea, looked, I cruelly observed, like a satellite encircling the sun.

What had I ever seen in her? I asked myself. She was, in a word, enormous.

And then they looked round and saw me.

'Carl! Hallo!' Cera spoke first, her wide mouth smiling in surprise and gladness. Greg, close by her side, nodded, smiling an echo of her smile. He had lost a number of teeth, I noticed. At their insistence I joined them and together we talked for some minutes. I learned that they had bought a house very close to the sea – a large, very old house. No, Cera said, they had no children. I thought she spoke with a touch of sadness in her voice. She must have heard it herself, for she added quickly:

'We don't need children. We don't need anyone. We have each other.'

I found myself grinning and nodding like a marionette. The very thought of them being so close to each other, so content in each other's company, was somehow sickening to me; the smile was all I could manage.

When it was time for them to go they made me promise that I would visit them one day. Cera wrote out their address and gave it to me.

'Any time,' she insisted. 'We hardly ever go out ourselves. Please come.'

Again I nodded my agreement, having not the slightest intention of ever keeping to it. I watched as Greg got up and helped Cera to her feet. She moved slowly, shifting her enormous bulk without grace, looking like some huge, stranded sea creature. I was reminded again of the angler fish and her tiny mate as Greg moved around her, before her, and again in her wake, his movements quick and sharp, his eyes never wavering, never moving from the great bulk of his adored wife.

All the hatred I had harboured for so long was now, I discovered, mixed with an unbelievable feeling of disgust and revulsion. I felt it hit me, sweep over me like a wave.

For some moments after they had gone I sat quite still. My coffee lay cold and forgotten before me, my sandwich drying on its plate. After a while I got up and, as if in a daze, moved away. My footsteps, I found, were leading me back to the Fish Gallery.

*The whole room is ablaze now. No one could possibly get to them . . .*

I did visit them eventually. At the time I told myself that it was because I was in the vicinity of Thorsall Down. But that's not really true. I know it now. I wanted to see them. I had to. Ever since the day in the Natural History Museum I had found myself devoured by a desire to see them again . . . Cera and Greg . . . those repulsive objects of my growing hatred.

I found the house without difficulty. It stood high up on the cliff overlooking the sea. The only approach to the front door was by means of a narrow pathway that wound through a wild, tangled garden, formless and unkempt. The hard, late November winds had all but stripped the trees of their last leaves, and as I stepped from my car I wondered how anyone could find pleasure in such a bleak, forbidding atmosphere.

With my collar pulled up high about my ears I made my way along the path to the old porch. My ring at the bell was answered by an old woman who took my name and retreated quickly into the shadows. Moments later she was back and ushering me into a large, warm room. Giving me a nod and a rather uncertain smile, she left me. And then Cera and Greg appeared.

The light in the room was quite dim but I could see well enough that in the six months since our last meeting the couple had changed even more.

I found myself wondering whether the drastic changes would have taken place had they never met each other. If Cera had married *me* would she still have become this gross, obscene creature that I now saw before me? Would Greg, left to his life in his hometown, still have developed into this little toothless, quick-moving caricature of a man?

Cutting into my thoughts came Cera's precise accents as she asked if I would stay for dinner. Taken by surprise, I heard myself accept her invitation, cursing inwardly a second later, for there was nothing I wanted more than to say my hurried goodbyes and go.

I eventually left after about two hours. They had to be the longest two hours of my life.

For what seemed ages after the front door closed behind me I remember standing at the end of the long garden path breathing in the clear autumn air in great gulps. Clutching the handle of my car door I fought against the nausea that arose in me. My eyes clenched as tightly as my fists, I tried to dispel the images that swam in my mind, threatening to swamp me. But the pictures wouldn't go. I watched all over again as Greg sat at the table – so close to Cera that their bodies often touched – eating from a bowl a mess of soggy, sloppy pap that she had served him.

'Poor darling cannot chew since he lost all his teeth,' she explained with loving sympathy in her voice.

She and I ate some dish of meat and vegetables. I ate without tasting a mouthful, so desperately eager was I to get away.

But for the moment there was no escape. I was forced to watch as Cera picked up a spoonful of the slop from Greg's dish and fed him, gently pushing the bowl of the wooden spoon between his thick, fleshy lips, past his pink, toothless gums. He slobbered, nestling into her gigantic bosom, the food dribbling down over his weak chin as if he no longer had complete control over himself. And Cera didn't seem bothered in the least; she appeared to be as fond, as adoring of him as ever. The spectacle was sickening.

Later, as I headed back to London, I said to myself that two such hideous people should not be allowed to go on living . . .

*I had to do it. I had no choice. I only hope that no one will ever know. I pray it. But the fire must make sure of it . . . The fire. Nothing can be seen inside the room now . . . only the flames. The flames are everywhere . . .*

Of course I went back again. I had sworn to myself that I never would, but of course I did. I knew I would. I had to.

It was March when I retraced my steps along the narrow, winding garden path. As before, I had made no announcement of my impending arrival and I thought, just for a moment, that they had gone away; I could see no lights shining through the curtains. It was with some relief that I heard the footsteps coming to answer my ring at the door. In another two minutes I was being shown into the lounge by the old servant I had seen previously. When she had gone I sat down, waiting patiently for Cera and Greg to come in and greet me.

The room was large and lit only by the firelight and one small lamp. Outside, a wind had sprung up, buffeting the house in its exposed position, crying round the corners. Its sound made a forlorn, melancholy background to the bright crackle of the burning log in the grate. And then came the sound of Cera's voice.

'It's nice to see you, Carl. And such a surprise. Come and sit over here by me.'

Having turned in the direction of her voice I at last made out her shape as she lounged in the shadows.

'Hallo, Cera . . .'

I moved to her and sat in the chair which she indicated. Before me her huge bulk was draped over a red velvet couch, the legs of which must surely have been groaning beneath her weight. I studied her in the fitful glow of the fire.

There was no longer even the remotest trace of the girl I had met in Regent Street all those empty, unhappy years ago.

She bore hardly any likeness to a woman at all now, and I shuddered to imagine what she must look like divested of her clothing. Her shape was not smooth as one might have expected, but oddly lumpy, and the flickering firelight playing on the great mound of her body gave, I thought, beneath the folds of her loose robe, the strange impression of movement.

I looked at her face. Her mouth with its strong, sharp white teeth looked wider than before, while her little round eyes, set in the increasing expanse of her pale flesh, seemed almost to have disappeared. I looked away again.

'Where is Greg?' I asked.

For a long moment she hesitated, then she said:

'He is away.' A pause, then she added: 'It is a pity you cannot see him. He will be sorry to have missed you.'

I was about to ask more specifically where he was when she forestalled me with a question of her own.

'Did you come by train?'

'No. By car again. I parked it on the road like last time. I could find no garage or any other suitable spot.'

'There is none.' She shook her head and her whole body seemed to quiver.

'Then where do you keep *your* car?'

'We have no need of a car,' she answered. 'We have no need to go anywhere. Everything we need is here. Whatever provisions we require are brought to the house. And we have our servants. We manage very well.' After a pause, she added – with, I thought, a trace of smugness – 'We are very self-sufficient here.'

At this point the maid came to the door and announced that if nothing more was wanted then she and the cook would like to leave for the night.

'Thank you, dear.' Cera smiled. 'We'll see you in the morning.'

When the maid had gone Cera said with a shrug:

'It is impossible to get servants to live in . . .'

'It must be expensive, running a large house like this,' I said, '– servants as well . . .'

'Oh, well –' another smile, showing her white teeth – 'as I said before, we manage.'

I realized suddenly how very little I knew about her. What was her background? Obviously she had considerable wealth;

neither she nor Greg seemed to have done a stroke of work since their marriage.

'Are you surprised to see me?' I asked.

'No.' She shook her head. 'I thought you would come again.'

'Are you sorry I came?'

She looked away from me. She spoke softly.

'Perhaps it would be better if you did not come back . . .'

'Yes . . .' She was right. In a moment, I determined, I would get up, go, and never come back. What was I doing here now? I asked myself. It was insane. I rose to my feet and picked up my coat. 'No, please,' I said, gesturing as she began to move her great bulk off the couch. 'I can see myself out.'

'Nonsense. We can't forget our manners. We'll see you to the door.'

As she got to her feet I could see at last just how enormous she had become. She must be pregnant, I thought . . . unless she were very ill . . . But it was not her weight alone. Surely she was now taller than I. The level of her small, button-like eyes was higher than my own. Looking down I tried to see whether she was wearing high-heels, but the length of her robe hid her feet from view. Beneath her robe I became aware once more of that flickering of life, a pulsating that must be, I told myself, a trick of the light.

'Goodbye, Cera . . .'

'Goodbye, Carl . . . Perhaps some day you will understand . . .'

Never, I said to myself.

'Well . . . ' Cera put out her hand and, hesitating for the briefest moment, I took it. The feel of her flesh was cool and clammy. Quickly I released her and then, much relieved, moved to the door. Behind me she followed, moving slumberously, tortuously, her great, unwieldy body swaying with her slow, graceless steps. And then the door was opening and I was out into the air again, hurrying away down the path, back to normality. I could feel Cera's eyes upon me as I went. As I reached a corner I turned and looked back; she was still there, framed in the soft light of the doorway, looking like a monstrous, grotesque museum specimen.

My sleep that night was fitful. I awoke many times, and each time, it seemed, Cera's body was there before me; and then Greg, small and insignificant in the shadow of her overpowering bulk. And even in my dreams she was there, swimming by, floating by, the folds of her loose, voluminous robes drifting, undulating, twitching around her. In the morning I got up thick-headed, and unsteady on my feet from lack of sleep.

I went through my day at school with my mind only half on my job. And all the while my thoughts of Cera and Greg were lurking there, ready to take over. I grew more and more obsessed with them with every passing hour.

I put my obsession down to the fact that, quite simply, they needed *explaining*. It was just that. They were beyond my understanding, and I couldn't let such a mystery rest. Had they always been quite so grotesque, always so repellent? Was the change in them existing only in my own imagination? There were so many questions. When I got back to my flat later that afternoon I at once searched for the newspaper clippings that I had kept for so long. I smoothed at the yellowing photograph and looked at the smiling faces there. They looked young and happy. Cera's smile was dazzling, and there below was Greg's happy face as she towered above him like some giant protectress.

I turned to the newsprint and read again the words that had, at one time, so devastated my own happiness:

'. . . at the marriage of Mr Gregory Marchant and his bride, the former Miss Cera Tiidae . . .'

'Tiidae . . . ' I said the name aloud. And I recalled my own words when she had first told me her name: 'What kind of a name is that?' I had asked jokingly. Cera . . . Tiidae . . . Cera Tiidae . . . In my mind the names rolled around, moving, shifting . . . It was almost as if my brain wanted only the merest jolt for the pieces to fall into place . . . Cera . . . Tiidae . . . It meant something to me – if only I could find what it was.

Casting my mind back I searched my experiences for a clue. There was something there – I knew it – something that would give my mind the necessary jolt. It was something connected with one of our meetings . . . The beach . . . No . . . Where else had we met? At their house in Thorsall Down and in the cafeteria of the museum . . .

Click. It was the proverbial piece of puzzle falling into place. *If* I was right.

No. *No!* I must be mistaken, I told myself. I must be wrong!

The whole idea, the whole conception, was too dreadful to contemplate.

When the Natural History Museum opened this morning I was waiting on the steps. I had already telephoned the headmaster of my school to say that I might be a little late. Now, hurrying past the surprised doormen, I went at once to the gallery where the fish exhibits were kept. There, striding purposefully between the rows of glass cases, I came at last to the end where the model of the angler fish was kept.

My heart pounding, I stared at the grotesque creatures. There was the enormous female with the wide mouth and the tiny button-like eyes. And there was the male, so small in comparison. And there, beside them, was the name: *Ceratias holboelli (family: Ceratiidae)* . . . *Ceratiidae* . . . Cera Tiidae . . .

But how could it be? How was it possible? That was something I would never know, I was certain. I was only sure that it was so . . . I found myself holding on to the sides of the case for support. My head was so low that my breath was misting the glass. I shook myself and stood straight. I must be living in some terrible nightmare. Soon I would awaken, relieved beyond measure to have escaped such awful reality.

But I knew it was no dream. Trembling slightly, I went on to read the rest of the neatly-printed information. It explained many things: the absence of Greg, the strange movements beneath her robe, her grossness, and slowness of gait . . .

In the men's lavatory a few minutes later I was violently sick. Afterwards I phoned the school again, this time to tell them I would not be in. Then, with my new-found knowledge, I drove back to Wimbledon where I sat in my kitchen for long hours over numerous cigarettes and cups of coffee. Very late in the afternoon I came to a decision. I would go back. Quickly I got into my car and drove away.

It was quite dark when at last I parked my car and walked up the garden path. The servants would have left by now, I thought. I was glad of that. Ahead of me the large house was, as before, quite quiet. I rang the bell and waited.

I rang again.

After ten minutes of ringing and waiting it was obvious to me that there would be no answer. I tried the door, found it opened to my touch, and went in.

Entering the lounge I found a bright fire burning in the

hearth; the top log had only just caught, so it was clear that the room had very recently been vacated.

'Cera . . . ?'

I waited, listening, but there was no reply to my call.

The french windows leading to the cliff-top were wide open. I crossed the room and stood, breathing in the salt, night air. Below me the sea stretched away into the distance, dark, mysterious, hiding who-knew-what unbelievable, unfathomable secrets.

Moving quickly down the shallow steps I went out on to the hard, rocky surface and looked down. The moon had risen, its light sparking off the waves as they broke over the stones at the foot of the cliff.

For some minutes I remained there, peering out across the water, my eyes straining in the light. And then, with a start, I saw them.

Frantically, nervously, I searched about me till I had located the head of a narrow path leading to the beach below. Hurrying, and careless of my safety, I scrambled down, almost falling in my anxiety to reach the bottom.

At the water's lapping edge I stood, watching and waiting. Nearby on a large rock was draped her robe; I knew she would soon come to shore.

And there she was. Suddenly. Just thirty yards away, her head breaking the waves in the path of the moon's reflection. As yet she had not caught sight of me. I knew it would be just a matter of seconds before she did, though, and I prayed that first of all I would have a chance to *see*. I had to know. For certain. The next moment I did.

As I watched, holding my breath, she found her footing in the sand and heaved her huge body out of the water. And for one brief, dazzlingly-clear instant I saw them. In the same second she saw *me*.

*'Carl!'*

My name issuing from her lips was nearly a scream. It was followed almost at once by a loud splash as she threw herself back into the sea, taking cover beneath its darkened surface. I did not move.

'Carl . . . ?'

Looking over to my right I saw her head above the waves.

'Yes . . . ?'

'Please,' she said, '. . . close your eyes. Just for a moment.

With my eyes tight shut I waited. Her voice came again, closer at hand now.

'All right.'

I saw that she was standing about five yards away from me. We faced each other across the sand. The robe that had lain on the rock was now clutched tightly to her body.

'Thank you,' she said quietly.

'It doesn't matter,' I said. 'I saw.'

'Yes.' She nodded and turned her head away from me. 'I didn't want you to. I had hoped – we had hoped – that no one would ever know.'

'It suddenly came to me,' I said. 'Quite by chance. The idea. Then I made it my business to find out. For certain. I had to.'

'And what will you do – now that you know?' She was staring at me intently now.

'I hated you,' I said for answer. 'Both of you. I wanted so desperately to hurt you. As I had been hurt.'

'That was a long time ago.'

'Yes. But some injuries take longer to heal.' I paused briefly, then, my voice even, I added:

'You disgust me.'

She flinched slightly as if I had struck her. Her body shook. Long moments of silence went by, and she repeated her question.

'What are you going to do, Carl?'

Suddenly, she was crying. Tears spilled from her small, round eyes and trickled down her wide, fleshy cheeks. I wished I had never come. If only I could have been content with *not knowing* . . . But it was too late for that. Turning quickly I strode back in the direction of the cliff path. Behind me her voice cried out in sudden anguish.

'Carl! Wait!'

I walked on.

'Carl! Please! What are you going to do?'

I wouldn't listen. Mentally shutting my ears to the sound I hurried over the sand. Reaching the path, I began to clamber up. Behind me the sound of her sobs punctuated her laboured breathing as she strove to catch up. Looking over my shoulder I saw her as, clutching her body, she stumbled along in my wake, her voice, hollow with fear, crying out again and again.

I was half-way up the cliff path when I heard her pleadings turn to a scream of terror and pain. I spun. Looking down

I saw her where she had fallen, lying sprawled out in the moonlight. In seconds I was at her side.

'Are you all right?' I knelt in the sand, anxiously watching the pain fleeting in spasms across her face.

'I think so.' She spoke as if with effort.

'Both of you?'

'I think so.' She stiffened for a split-second, grimacing as a sudden stab of pain caught at her breath. With her hands and arms she hugged her body, protective, comforting. 'Help me. Please,' she said.

Steadying her enormous weight as best I could, I helped her to her feet. How we made it to the top of the cliff I shall never know. But somehow we managed it. Panting, gasping for breath I helped her up the steps and in through the french windows. There, as if every ounce of her strength had been used, she collapsed, falling on the floor in a heap.

'Cera . . . Cera . . .' I was by her again, reaching out to her, touching her cold, clammy skin. 'I'm sorry,' I murmured. 'I'm sorry.'

'It doesn't matter now.' She tried to smile at me but somehow the smile didn't quite work. 'It'll be all right,' she said.

Her robe had fallen open when she fell, and in the flickering glow from the fire I could see clearly the small body of her mate. His arms and legs wrapped around her, he clung there, his head just above the level of her great pendulous breasts. I remembered what I had read in the museum. I knew that, if I looked more closely, I would see that his mouth had joined itself to her flesh, the skin of his large lips fusing with *her* skin, his blood supply coming directly from her own. No longer having any life of his own, Greg had become completely parasitic, depending upon his mate for the gift of life itself.

I wondered why it is that parasites should appear so physically loathsome? Greg was no exception. Bearing absolutely no resemblance to any human form he held on to his saviour, his lover, his wife. He looked like nothing so much as a grotesque, monstrous, cancerous growth.

'Carl . . .' Cera had seen the expression in my eyes. 'Don't look like that,' she said softly. 'We are what we are . . .'

'I'm sorry.'

'Cover us, please . . .'

I wrapped the robe around her, around them both. It wasn't the warmth that she was seeking, I thought, but privacy from my shocked, commenting gaze. After a moment she said:

'I am hurt, Carl . . . The fall . . .' She winced as a stab of agony underlined her words and a little bubble of blood formed from the corner of her mouth, became a trickle and ran down to disappear beneath the collar of her robe.

'I could get a doctor,' I suggested, knowing that the idea was ridiculous. She shook her head.

'No. No doctor. There are some things that should always be secret.'

And then she was turning, trying to lie on her side, the blood gushing out of her mouth and her nose, her small, fish-like eyes rolling in her head. Underneath the fabric of her robe I was aware of a sudden movement. It was Greg, beginning his own futile fight for survival. It wouldn't last long, I knew.

I knelt at Cera's side, quite helpless in the face of her desperation. How she fought! How she struggled to cling to her unlovely existence.

But at last it was over.

For some moments after Cera died, Greg continued with his small, jerky movements, till in the end they faded and grew still. I rose to my feet, my knees stiff from the period of kneeling. Below me in a pool of blood lay Cera's body, her arms still shielding the degenerate form of her mate as, clutched to her still breast, he lay upon her.

I couldn't leave them like that, I decided, and recalled her words that some things are best left secret. It is true. Particularly such a secret as hers. It was as I lit a cigarette with an ember from the fire that the thought came to me. I debated only for seconds before making my decision. It is final . . .

The curtains caught so easily, the flames running straight up to lick at the low-beamed ceiling. It won't take long at all, I thought . . .

*There is no one about. In this desolate spot it seems that more than a fire is needed to attract attention. But someone will be along sooner or later. Perhaps I won't bother to telephone the fire brigade after all. What can they do? Nothing. It would serve no purpose. Anything that mattered was beyond all earthly control a long, long time ago . . .*

# LOST SOUL

*Pamela Vincent*

Alfred liked the laundromat. It was warm and friendly, and there was usually someone ready to talk while the machines did their work.

He didn't have enough to make up a load himself very often but there was nothing to stop him sitting there just the same, and when he didn't have his own laundry to look after it gave him more time for other people's, so that he could keep an eye open for the warning red light of something wrong, while a customer slipped out for ten minutes.

He didn't make a nuisance of himself, of course, boring folk to death or forcing them into conversation when they wanted to read the paper or anything, but some of them were glad of a willing ear to listen to their troubles – it's easier to talk to a stranger than your own family about some things, and families aren't interested anyway. He'd heard all sorts of queer stories that way, like the man who . . . But he didn't pass on what he heard; that's why they knew they could talk to him.

It made him feel almost like a priest, except that he wasn't a Catholic. Wasn't anything, really. Oh, he believed in going to heaven after you were dead, or the other place, but that was all to do with how you lived, whether you lived right and helped your neighbour, that sort of thing. He didn't think he'd have to worry when the time came, and Doris would look after him the way she had when they'd been together. She'd be there waiting to guide him.

Tonight the laundromat was pretty quiet, probably because it was raining heavily. The windows were steamed up, enclosing them within a warm little cocoon which hummed gently from the two or three machines that were working. Alfred had no one to talk to at the moment but he rather enjoyed being able to watch the kaleidoscope of patterns and colours churning away behind each glass porthole. Not so much the washing-machines, mostly smothered in suds, but the drying-machines with their big windows. Some folk were lucky, they had multi-striped sheets – he and Doris had never dreamt of anything other than good, plain white, so serviceable that they were never going to wear out in Alfred's lifetime. Would all those colours have made any difference to their married life, he wondered? Maybe they'd have spent more time in bed . . .

Naturally, he pretended not to look when people were loading and unloading the machines, as he hoped they avoided watching him. It was embarrassing to have all your little secrets on show like that, the mends and the bits that needed mending, the working-clothes that were too shamefully dirty, or the old-fashioned garments that others would find funny. Some of the underwear nowadays – whew! Both male and female, a lot more daring than he and Doris could have imagined, much less bought and worn.

Someone was using the dry-cleaning machine, if you could call it 'dry' when it is so obviously wet inside there. Alfred drew closer, shifting cautiously along the bench that lined the wall.

A very interesting combination, everything black or white or grey, or a mixture of these. Fascinated, he watched them whirling, tossed like the souls in Dante's 'Inferno'. They were all there, just like human life, the bad and the good rubbing shoulders with the not-so-bad or not-so-good, or those that were sometimes one, sometimes the other. Twisting up together, recoiling from one another, swimming in the pool of worldly temptation or flying in the cleansing wind of redemption. And at the end they'd all come out purified but the same as they went in: black, white, grey. Just like human life.

He was almost disappointed when the owner came to claim them. There they were, suits and dresses and trousers once again, their souls washed away with the city grime.

He couldn't tell her about his odd fancies; she didn't look the sort of girl who'd understand. Probably think him a crackpot and rush away too soon, before the chemical fumes had safely evaporated, so that she'd be overcome inside the car, shut in against the beating rain.

There he went again, creating a whole sequence of events out of nothing, condemning the poor girl to death because she'd unwittingly cheated him out of his souls serving their time in Purgatory – that was more like it, Purgatory, another Catholic idea but not one he normally subscribed to. Still, it seemed to fit the case this time, the way the dirty souls emerged clean and refreshed, no more sin or sorrow to take into their new lives.

She gathered them up at last, carefully covering them with polythene before dashing out to the car park at the rear, and now Alfred noticed that nearly everyone else had gone; there was only one old lady left. She'd been looking at a book: looking at it, not reading it. Alfred hadn't seen her turn a page – she'd been staring at the same one the whole time she'd been sitting down. He knew because there was some sort of fancy chapter heading. Her face was closed and set. Troubled, but there was no way Alfred could make a tactful approach. She never even gave him a glance so that he could remark on the unseasonal weather or ask her opinion of the book. He was disappointed when she rose immediately the machine stopped; he'd hoped to be able to draw her attention to it and start a conversation that way. Poor old soul, she needed help if he could think of some means of giving it to her.

He watched her choosing a drying-machine, peering inside each one and feeling with her hands to make sure they were clean. She must have been caught like he was once, when some idiot had left a sticky mess to spoil the next unwary user's clean laundry. Or, like him, she may have been looking for a machine with some heat left over. She finally wheeled her trolley over and started loading carefully, as if she were trying to spin the job out as long as possible.

'Giving it all her attention,' Alfred told himself, 'to take her mind off her trouble, whatever it is.'

He could see her profile, still cast in its lines of sorrow, and his heart ached for her. Poor, unhappy soul, seeking solace if not salvation. She was bending her old bones right inside the interior of the machine, still hot from its last use, smoothing out the items at the back.

It was the easiest thing in the world to lift her in a little farther – she was so pitifully small and light after a lifetime of deprivation – and he didn't grudge the coin that would purge her soul of its suffering.

He set the dial to HOT as he firmly closed the door.

# IF THY RIGHT HAND OFFEND THEE...

*A. E. Ellis*

*In view of disquieting rumours which have come to his notice, relating to certain unusual occurrences at St Chrysostom's College last Michaelmas Term, the Headmaster feels compelled to make public the following Report, which to the best of his belief is an accurate and trustworthy record of what took place. This has been done with the consent of the Medical Officer, who agrees that the good name of the school must not be prejudiced by the exaggerated and damaging fabrications at present current.*

Report of the Resident Medical Officer at St Chrysostom's College to the Headmaster and Governors of the College, December 1925.

Gentlemen,

In the course of my annual Report on the state of health of the School, I had occasion to allude to a puzzling case of fever, therein stated to be 'possibly a form of recurrent malaria', but which in truth even so eminent an authority as Sir Humphrey Chambers was unable to diagnose with anything approaching confidence. I accordingly beg to lay before you the following narrative, as the extraordinary occurrences which I am about to relate, although outside the scope of medical practice, appear to have a bearing on this curious case.

The case in question first came to my notice when the telephone in my private room in college rang at about 5.30 p.m. on Sunday, 25th October, and I was urgently summoned by the Matron in charge of the sanatorium to attend to a boy who had just been brought in by his companions and who was becoming delirious.

On reaching the sanatorium, which as you are aware is situated some two hundred yards from the main College buildings, at the end of an avenue of beech trees, I found the boy, Richard Henryson, in bed, restless and feverish and unable to speak coherently. I at first thought it might be a case of pneumonia, but the boy's lungs proved to be sound and, so far as could be ascertained, he suffered from no organic disorder. Concluding that he must have contracted a sudden chill on the liver, I prescribed appropriate treatment and left.

The following incident may appear trivial and irrelevant, but in the light of subsequent events I am inclined to attach to it some significance.

On returning down the avenue from the sanatorium, I had a quite definite feeling that someone was moving along parallel with me a few yards to the rear, hidden from sight by the trees. As this seemed unusual, I paused to allow this person to overtake me, in order to see who it was. That it was unlikely to be one of the boys I knew, for they were then at evensong in the College chapel. Whoever was there, however, did not appear, so I walked on a few paces and then abruptly faced about.

Ten yards off, standing with one hand on the bole of a beech, stood a figure, whether male or female I could not discern in the dim light, attired in what looked like a thin coat or mackintosh, with some sort of scarf or shawl enveloping the head. The coat and shawl struck me as odd, for it had been a sunny autumn day and the air was still warm. The figure made no movement, so I called out, 'Who is there?' and took a pace nearer. The person instantly dodged behind the tree and made off up the avenue at some speed, though it appeared to glide rather than to run. I started to give chase but soon found myself outdistanced. Concluding that the stranger must be some vagrant on the look-out for pickings around the College, I went back to my rooms and soon forgot about the incident.

After supper that day three boys came to see me, saying they wished to make a statement about Henryson, with whom they had spent the afternoon. The four of them had gone to Hoecourt Ring, the site of a Romano-British temple in the neighbourhood, where they had lain down to rest. Doubtless prompted by the mystical associations of the place, they had started talking about ghosts and spiritualism, and finally, as a sort of game, decided to hold a seance.

The boys sat round in a circle in the middle of the Ring and one of them, a tall, dark youth of arresting appearance, commenced to make hypnotic passes over Henryson, who is a slim, sensitive boy of a rather girlish type. At first they treated the proceedings as a jest and there was a good deal of laughter. Then Henryson seemed to grow sleepy and they thought he was pretending to fall into a hypnotic trance. Presently the boy started muttering to himself and his eyes acquired an unnaturally intent expression. This startled his companions, who told him not to look like a stuffed owl, and one of them gave him a shake. This produced no effect, and Henryson soon lost consciousness and lolled back against a tree.

At this point in his narrative, the boy who was acting as spokesman hesitated and looked somewhat embarrassed, as if there was something more which he was reluctant to mention. I urged them to relate everything that had occurred, and each boy admitted that he had felt just then as if someone else was present with them – 'somebody who ought not to have been there,' as one of them expressed it. Another boy remarked that he felt as he did once when he was smoking an illicit cigarette and suddenly became aware that his housemaster was watching him over the fence – 'only,' he added, 'it was far worse than that, very much worse.' They could see no one about, however, and as Henryson now seemed to be really ill, they carried him in scared silence across the two or three fields between Hoecourt Ring and the College sanatorium. That was all they could tell me, except that Henryson had been in perfect health and high spirits before their seance.

On Monday Henryson's condition had worsened; he had become delirious and was getting difficult to control. Accordingly I called in the eminent specialist, Sir Humphrey Chambers, who, after a thorough examination of the patient, was obliged to confess himself puzzled by the symptoms. Febrifuges were prescribed, but we both felt far from satisfied with the nature of the case. It was decided not to send the boy to hospital, so that I could maintain direct observation, and a night-nurse was engaged.

In relating the following episodes, I am fully aware that my professional reputation is imperilled, yet I do so in the conviction that these incredible events are not unrelated to the mysterious complaint of my patient.

Mr Matthews, the biology master, was accustomed to working late in the evening in his laboratory, which is situated at a little distance from the main College buildings, and is almost overshadowed by the avenue of trees leading to the sanatorium. One night – it was the last day of October – as Mr Matthews was walking across to his laboratory, he noticed somebody attired in what appeared to be a faded mackintosh standing under the trees and looking towards him. The face was in shadow, and Mr Matthews, thinking it might be a College servant, called out in his friendly manner, 'What a delightful evening!' The person took no notice, so Mr Matthews, out of curiosity to see who it might be, turned aside so as to pass nearer.

At that moment a light was switched on in one of the rooms of the College and the beam from the open window fell on the face of the figure under the trees. Mr Matthews stopped dead, for he beheld, not the features of anyone he knew, but the grinning face of a skull – yet not merely a skull, for there were some parched and blackened remnants of skin drawn over it, adding to the unutterable horror of the thing.

For some moments Mr Matthews stood petrified. Then a probable explanation occurred to him, and his terror gave place to wrath, for he remembered that this was All Hallows E'en, and concluded that some mischievous boys must have removed the mounted skeleton from the biology laboratory, dressed it up and played this ghastly trick on him. Having reached this solution, he was about to approach for a closer inspection when the thing moved, stretched out its right hand and moved towards him.

Mr Matthews turned and ran, with the grisly horror at his heels. Fortunately the door of the laboratory stood open. He dashed through and slammed it behind him with a crash and the spring lock clicked home. But something had dropped behind him inside the door as it shut. Groping for the switch he turned on the light and saw, lying just within the door, a dead and bony hand.

This was too much for Mr Matthews. Through the frosted glass of the door he could see that the Thing was still outside, fumbling at the door as though trying to open it. Mr Matthews crossed to the other side of the laboratory, opened a casement window and, with a backward glance to make sure that his pursuer was still outside the door, jumped out and raced for his rooms in the College. He dared not glance back, nor did he dare to tell anyone of his macabre encounter, as he was sure to be disbelieved and would be thought drunk or mad.

Next morning when Mr Matthews cautiously entered his laboratory, the hand had gone and there was no trace of his ghastly visitor. But perhaps it is scarcely accurate to say *no* trace, for caught on the fastener of the window, which he had left open in his escape the previous night, was a ragged strip of greyish cloth with an unwholesome, earthy smell. This, however, may merely have been a piece of one of the laboratory assistant's dusters.

Mr Matthews was destined to see his grim visitant again, three days after his harrowing experience on the eve of All Saints. Having somewhat recovered confidence, he had ventured across to his laboratory after dinner at about 8.30 p.m., and was occupied on a dissection for demonstration to a class next day. Presently he heard someone moving about in the next room, but was surprised not to see any light. As he was about to investigate, the door of his laboratory opened and the grisly apparition, from which he had fled a few evenings before, entered the room and came towards him.

Mr Matthews was overcome with horror and revulsion as he stood fascinated by the menacing advance of this hideous spectre. The Thing seemed to be beseeching him to do something for it. Its dead face was thrust close to Mr Matthews, and he observed that it carried its severed right hand in a fold of its cloak, which was nothing other than a winding-sheet. With its left hand the Thing pointed to Mr Matthews's right hand, in which he still held a pair of dissecting scissors, and opened its mouth as if to speak, though no sound came out of those gaping, lipless jaws.

Mr Matthews stood paralysed. Exasperated by his unresponsiveness, the Thing appeared to grow angry, and what Mr Matthews afterwards described as an oppressive sense of evil intent emanated from it. It raised its bony left hand, seized Mr Matthews by the jaw and, wrenching his mouth open, grasped hold of his tongue. At this fearful moment Mr Matthews heard voices outside, which he recognized as those of two of his sixth-form pupils who were coming for private tuition. His grim assailant evidently heard them too, for it hastily left Mr Matthews, went out through an open window and vanished, just as the boys came in to find the biology master lying in a faint, his face scratched and bleeding.

I was immediately summoned, but although Mr Matthews soon recovered consciousness, his tongue was too sore and swollen to allow him to speak or to eat for some days. However, he wrote an account of this and also of his previous encounter, which he placed at my disposal. So broken down was he by these terrifying and inexplicable experiences that he was obliged to go away for a fortnight to recuperate. By the time he returned the College had ceased to be troubled by an unearthly visitant.

On the evening of the second day after the last visitation of Mr Matthews, I was sitting in my study in College, engaged in polishing some of my surgical instruments. The casement window stood wide open, as it was a calm night, and everything was very quiet, the boys all being in evening preparation. Hearing a slight noise behind me, I glanced round and perceived someone just inside the window, partly hidden by the curtains. I had just been reading Mr Matthews's extraordinary narrative, so I arose in some alarm and turned the reading-lamp so that its light fell on the intruder.

There it stood, the same gruesome Thing that Mr Matthews had described, and the very same, I feel certain, as the person I had seen lurking in the sanatorium avenue on the Sunday when Henryson fell ill. I shouted in alarm and backed towards the door, but as my rooms are in a lonely wing of the College, my cries were unheard. The Thing then moved rapidly between me and the door, and with a wave of its shrouded arms it drove me, shrinking with fear and horror, towards the table on which lay my surgical instruments. Pointing to one of the larger scalpels, it drew near and held its hideous mummy of a face within a few inches of mine, with its mouth open and its withered tongue protruding as though in obscene mockery. I stood bewildered and horrified, while experiencing a sensation of terror such as I had never before known.

The Thing seemed to radiate evil. I cannot hope to convey in words the feeling of deadly menace that overpowered me while confronting this loathsome corpse. All the time it seemed to be striving to get me to do something for it, and indicated my surgical instruments with impatient gestures of its left hand. Its right hand had been severed at the wrist, and I could see its claw-like fingers protruding from a fold in the cerement. I was incapable of action, however, and felt that the Thing would soon become actively malevolent and attack me, even as it had assaulted Mr Matthews. This I consider would indeed have occurred, had not the boys at that moment been released from evening preparation, and the noise of their shouting as they ran along the corridor to the dormitories disturbed my visitor. With a final gesture of threatening appeal, it turned and disappeared through the window, which I hastily closed and fastened.

After this unnerving experience, I decided that Henryson's condition would warrant my vacating my own bedroom for the night and taking up quarters in the sanatorium, ostensibly to be on hand in case the patient became worse but in reality to be within sight and call of human beings.

On my way up the avenue I caught a glimpse of a shrouded figure approaching from the direction of the wing where my rooms are situated, but breaking into a run I reached the welcome sanctuary of the sanatorium without any further encounter.

Joshua Mullins, the College gardener, was walking homewards shortly after sunset on Friday, 6th November, after working late clipping the hedge bordering his chrysanthemum beds, which are situated some thirty yards from the sanatorium avenue. While pruning the hedge he had been vaguely aware of somebody watching him from the avenue, and concluded it must be some convalescent from the sanatorium who had nothing better to occupy him. Mullins finished trimming the hedge at sundown, and was taking his shears home with him, intending to clip the hedge of his own cottage next day. His homeward path led along the north-east and south-west sides of a broad, sloping meadow, in which a dozen bullocks were placidly grazing, and he noticed that the workmen, who had been digging a drain across the field, had gone home.

As he was turning the east corner of the field, Mullins observed someone who, as he could just make out in the fading light, was wearing some sort of long cloak or overall, start off from the upper, north corner of the field and move rapidly across the meadow so as to intercept him at the lower, south corner. Mullins supposed it must be some belated workman anxious not to miss the bus home, but was surprised to see the grazing cattle throw up their heads as the runner passed them and gallop with terrified snorts to the remotest corner of the field. Arrived at the south corner of the field, the figure halted and waited under the shadow of an elm for Mullins to come along. As the gardener reached the corner, the person lurking there stepped out to meet him.

It was with the utmost difficulty that I was able, weeks later, to persuade Mullins to tell me what it was that accosted him that evening. All he would or could say was that 'it was like someone who was dead, sir, almost a skelington, as you might say, only with something very nasty about it. And it never spoke, sir, but just came at me, and I backed against the fence. Then it reached out towards my shears, which I held in my left hand, and caught hold of my hand with its left hand and held it. Then I sort of dodged sideways and took the shears in my right hand and hurled them at it as hard as I could, so that the points stuck in its chest. Then it let go, and I set off running as hard as I could for a quarter of a mile till I got to the Packhorse Inn on the main road, where I went in and had a drop or two of something till I felt better, and then the bus came and I went home.'

On going to work next day, Mullins found his shears lying on the path at the spot where the encounter had taken place. Caught between the blades was a ragged piece of dirty cloth, which he gave me, and which Mr Matthews asserted to be of exactly the same material and sepulchral odour as the strip he had found on the laboratory window. Mullins was very careful after this adventure always to leave work while the light was still good, and showed an unwonted desire for company on his homeward walk.

The afternoon of the Sunday following the gardener's alarming experience was unusually mild and sunny for November. Miss Johnson, matron of one of the boarding houses, as she sat sewing at the window of her sitting-room, had been watching the bees flying in and out of the hives in the housemaster's garden, eager to make full use of this unexpected recrudescence of summer. But the brief spell of sunshine was now over, the bees had returned to their hives, and Miss Johnson, after observing the flocks of starlings flying in to roost in the beeches by the sanatorium, closed the window and resumed her needlework. The last rays of the setting sun dimmed into twilight and it became too dark to sew.

Miss Johnson, still holding a pair of scissors, rose to switch on the light, when she noticed someone standing outside the window looking in at her. Whoever it was realized that he had been seen, and motioned with his left hand, apparently indicating that she should open the window, and also kept pointing at the scissors she was holding. Before approaching the window, Miss Johnson switched on the light, which shone full on the face pressed against the pane. The matron gave a scream of terror and shut herself into her bedroom, where her maid, attracted by her cry, found her in hysterics on the bed, only able to repeat, 'The dead thing, mind the dead thing! Don't let it in!'

Next morning the bees from the hives below the matron's window were found dead and dying on the alighting boards.

I now come to the final episode in this amazing case, which took place on Wednesday, 11th November. I had been to the sanatorium to see Henryson, whose condition showed no improvement, although he had now been ill for two and a half weeks. At about 9.30 p.m. I went into the College library, in the forlorn hope of finding something to shed light upon his baffling complaint. As you are aware, the library is arranged on the plan of medieval libraries, with bookcases standing out at rightangles to the walls, forming recesses or bays, and opening off two of these bays are classrooms. As I sat turning over the pages of an encyclopædia, I heard a casement window banging now and then in one of these classrooms, and formed the intention of fastening it before leaving the library.

Presently I heard sounds as if someone was moving about in that classroom, and concluded that it must be Mr Heppelthwaite, the senior English master, preparing some work for next day. I was sitting some distance from the classroom, with my back towards its door, and did not trouble to look round when I heard someone come out and start pottering about at a shelf in the adjoining bay. The person then came down the centre of the library in my direction, moving a chair which blocked the way, so I called out, 'Hallo, Heppel, been burning the midnight oil?' As there was no answer to my jocular greeting, I turned round in some surprise – and there the Thing was, standing beside the table at which I sat.

My former horror returned and held me helpless. Rising shakily from the chair, I stared abjectly at the Thing's dead face, with its eyeless yet seeing sockets. With a swift movement it turned from me and bent down towards my surgical case, which I had brought with me from the sanatorium and laid on the table by my side. With its left hand it deftly unfastened the catch and then with a jerk scattered the instruments over the table. Then, selecting an operating scalpel, the creature advanced upon me. Fearing an attack, I shrank back against the bookcase, but it came on until we were about two feet apart and held out the knife, handle towards me, for me to take. This I did and stood sweating with fear, for the sense of evil which I had previously experienced in the presence of this Thing was now intensified and malignant.

The shrouded death now opened its lipless mouth, as it had done before, protruding its shrivelled and speechless tongue. I sensed that it urgently wanted me to do something for it. I could feel the intense, diabolical will of the Thing being exerted at me, overcoming my reason and governing my mind. That horrid tongue, lolling in the gruesome mouth, fascinated me, and all at once, moved by an uncontrollable impulse, I thrust the knife I held between those yawning jaws, with one frenzied stroke cut through the root of the tongue, then fell back, half fainting, into a chair.

The Thing picked up its severed tongue, wrapped it together with its amputated right hand in a fold of its winding-sheet, then turned towards me again. The change that had now come over this unearthly being was as amazing as anything in this extraordinary affair. Although its aspect underwent no change, yet I no longer felt that I was in the presence of some devilishly evil thing, but that it was filled with the happiness of some great joy, was a blessed spirit freed from some overwhelming trouble. Yet the Thing *looked* as foul and revolting as before; this radiant gladness was something far beyond its mutilated dead body.

The Thing then turned away and moved slowly to the end of the library, where stood a reading-desk on which lay a massive 1613 Bible. It stood before the lectern for some minutes with bowed head, then opened the book and turned over the pages until it reached some passage which appeared to rivet its attention, for it drew its finger along the lines as though reading. It then passed out through the doorway of the library and was never seen again.

When the transfigured being had thus departed, I went up to the Bible, which lay open at the fifth chapter of St Matthew's Gospel. After gazing for some time at the open pages, I noticed that the thirtieth verse had been underlined, as if with a none-too-clean finger-nail:

*'And if thy right hand offend thee, cut it off, and cast it from thee. For it is profitable for thee that one of thy members should perish, and not that thy whole body should be cast into hell.'*

What evil had that right hand done, that the unresting dead should thus return to harass mortal men? And the tongue, what heinous blasphemy had it spoken, that only by its extirpation could the lost soul be redeemed from the everlasting fire?

Some days after the final exit of the supernatural visitant whom, for lack of a better name, I have referred to as the Thing, the librarian discovered in the College library an ancient manuscript volume, dating from the sixteenth century, inscribed in barbarous Latin on vellum. The book was wedged between some little-read volumes on the divinity shelves, close to the door of the classroom where the Thing had effected its entry on its last visit. The book was not listed in the catalogue, and the librarian had never seen it before. Moreover, it was certainly not the kind of work that would ever be put in a school library, and it was indeed fortunate that it was inscribed in an archaic tongue and script. If any boy had got hold of the book and succeeded in deciphering its contents, I should be concerned for his peace of mind.

The book proved to be a treatise on sorcery and witchcraft written by one who was not only conversant with all the most nefarious branches of the black art, but, from the name on the title-page and the intimacy with which he treated the subject, was a leading exponent of these unhallowed practices. Those who have made a study of sorcery will be able to imagine something of what that book was like. I regret that I am unable to produce the obscene volume, as it would constitute valuable confirmatory evidence of the veracity of my Report, but the Chaplain, to whom I showed it, after translating a number of pages, was not to be restrained from putting it on the fire.

On looking up the trials for sorcery in the sixteenth century, it was found that the perpetrator of this infamous work met with retribution for his misdeeds and, as far as could be ascertained, suffered death at or near Hoecourt Ring. That he was not finally laid to rest until nearly four hundred years later this record tends to suggest.

There is but one more paragraph to add to my Report: on the night when the final visitation occurred, Henryson's condition began to improve. He slept peacefully and all signs of fever left him. Convalescence was swift, and within a week he was back in school.

## DISSOLVING PARTNERSHIP

*Martin Ricketts*

They were a remarkable pair. They lived in lodgings: adjoining rooms in Mrs Graham's Guest House, the ones with the low rent because of the continual noise from the shoe factory next door.

To an outsider they would have seemed less than partners. The elder of the two, the stout one with the penetrating eyes, grey moustache and cordial manner, appeared to be the boss. His name was Crowell.

The other one was a thin, anaemic little man by the name of Brooks. He never looked anyone straight in the face. His tiny, hedgehog eyes seemed to peer nervously from under his imperceptible eyebrows, his narrow chin jutting like a snout. The only person he ever really spoke to was Crowell – and even then he nearly always finished each sentence with 'sir'.

Crowell would have been a doctor, but he grew tired of his studies and gave it up. He had ideas of his own. During the year before he met Brooks, he would shut himself up in his room for days on end and fiddle with chemicals and peculiar apparatus. At times he would send out for ice or coal, at others for some strange concoctions from a private address in another part of the town. Whenever anyone spoke to him he would bow and smile and answer politely, but he never went out of his way to make conversation. He was clean and tidy, and he liked to keep his room that way, too. 'I don't know why I bother to go in and clean up,' Mrs Graham would say to her neighbours. 'It's always spotless in there, even the bench where he does his work. The tubes and jars gleam like diamonds, and everything is in its proper place. What? Of course I don't mind him using the room as a laboratory. He gets his gas and electricity off the coin-in-the-slot meters in his room and he pays his rent on time. That's all *I* worry about!'

Brooks turned up at about the same time that the room next door to Crowell's became vacant. Crowell introduced him to the place. Mrs Graham didn't like the look of the weaselly little man, but Crowell pacified her, saying that he and Mr Brooks were good friends and were going to be partners in business.

'I don't know what happened to Mr Rogers, the previous tenant,' Mrs Graham told her new lodger when she showed him into the room. 'He just up and vanished into thin air, didn't even take his belongings. Had to store 'em up downstairs. It's strange how he disappeared like that just as you was wanting a room. Sort of a lucky coincidence, eh? For you, I mean.'

Brooks nodded. He put his tiny suitcase down on the carpet and looked around the walls and up at the ceiling.

'Mr Crowell will pay my rent,' he muttered, then he closed the door in her face. That was the only time he ever spoke to her.

Often she would see the two of them together, whispering furtively on the stairs or standing outside on the pavement and gesturing at one another. After a few months she grew tired of wondering what kind of business they were partners in, and she ceased to listen for their footsteps on the stairs or their subdued, indistinct voices late at night. She soon took their strangeness for granted and left them to carry on with whatever affairs occupied their time.

For a few more months everything remained the same. Mrs Graham minded her own business, while Crowell and Brooks went out every evening and didn't come back until the early hours of the morning.

Then things began to change.

Crowell began to pace his room like a caged animal; at night Brooks would go out alone while he stayed behind to sweat and curse over his test-tubes and beakers. He refused to leave his room even for food, and Mrs Graham had to bring his meals to him on a tray. He lost weight and grew haggard; lack of sleep put dark rings under his eyes. Then one night he stopped cursing.

'I've done it, Brooks,' he whispered, laughing. 'By God, I've *done* it!'

'You have?' the little man said. It was two in the morning. He'd just returned from a job and he was tired.

'Take a look at this.' Crowell pointed at a shallow, glass-covered tray in which tiny creatures scurried around like insects.

'What are they?' Brooks asked as he craned forward. 'Ants?'

'No,' Crowell said. 'They're mice!'

'*Mice?*' The weaselly man pushed his face against the glass and frowned.

Crowell nodded. 'I've succeeded; I've made them smaller. You know what that means, don't you, Brooks?'

Brooks straightened and took a step backwards. 'Mr Crowell, I'm not sure that I . . .'

'Now, Brooks.' Crowell's face hardened. 'What do you think I've been working for, all these years? Don't tell me you've forgotten all the plans we made when we first talked about this partnership deal: I'll be the brains and you'll be the man of action. That's what we agreed, wasn't it?'

'But, Mr Crowell . . .'

'Listen, Brooks, this is going to make the Harrington job look like peanuts – and you remember how much we got for *those* jewels! Just think, we'll be able to break into the Campbell place and nobody will understand how it was done; they'll be *baffled*. All you have to do is drink some of this stuff and you'll shrink just like the mice. You'll be less than twelve inches tall and you'll be able to get through that tiny window in the toilet at the back of the shop . . . Then we'll be *rich*. We'll never have to do another job again!'

'And what about after?' Brooks said dubiously. 'Will you be able to get me back to my proper size again?'

Crowell smiled. 'Look at this.' He held up a beaker of milky liquid. 'This is the antidote. As soon as you finish the job you drink this and in no time at all you're back to how you were before.'

'But I don't understand it,' Brooks complained. 'Are you sure it's safe? How does it work?'

'It's quite simple really,' Crowell said patiently. 'It works by a process I've termed "molecular-contraction". Basically, it means that when you drink the stuff all the molecules in your body will sort of "pull together"; that is, they'll *contract*. Of course, there'll be problems, not the least of which is the fact that you'll be considerably smaller while still being the same weight as you are now, but we'll get over that . . .'

'I don't think . . .' Brooks began to tremble.

Crowell grabbed him by the collar. Brooks tried in vain to squirm away from the big man's penetrating stare. 'Listen, small fry,' Crowell said. 'I've been working on this for years, and I'm not going to let *you* cock it up. So, just to keep you happy, we're going to try it out here and *now*!'

All colour drained out of the little man's face. 'But I . . .'

Crowell let go of him, turned and picked up a beaker of liquid. He thrust it at Brooks. 'Here,' he said fiercely. '*Drink it!*'

The weaselly man closed his eyes, swallowed, then reached out for the beaker. He held it in front of him for a moment, his nose wrinkling, then suddenly he lifted his head, tilted the beaker over his mouth, and drank.

He put the beaker down slowly and waited. The two men gazed at each other silently, frozen like wax dummies. Then suddenly Brooks gave a little choked cry. He tottered, eyes rolling, then slumped forward on to his knees. Crowell stared; then he smiled. It was working! By God, it was *working*! The little man was growing *smaller*!

Brooks began to writhe, hands clutching. 'I feel strange,' he wailed.

Crowell bent over him, watching him shrink. In less than two minutes he was nearly half his normal size. His clothes, now ridiculously too large for him, hung from his limbs like heavy drapes.

Crowell knelt on the carpet. 'How do you feel now?'

'Frightened,' Brooks said in a squeaky voice as he struggled out of the suffocating expanse of his shirt.

Then Crowell frowned. The rate of shrinkage seemed to be increasing. But that was impossible; his calculations had definitely shown that it would remain constant!

'Something's gone wrong,' he said.

Brooks squeaked in panic. 'Do something!' he piped. '*Do something!*'

Crowell leapt to his feet. The antidote! He grabbed the second beaker and put it down on the floor. Brooks, now less than eighteen inches tall and completely naked, put his face down into the milky liquid and sipped.

Still he shrank.

'It's no good!' he squealed in desperation. 'It's no *good*!'

Crowell staggered back against the workbench. He reeled with panic. The tiny man, shrinking ever more rapidly, jumped up and down in front of him. Suddenly he knew. There was only one thing he *could* do to stop it. He heaved himself forward and swayed over the tiny gesticulating figure. He lifted his foot.

'Please don't step on me,' the tiny man squeaked in terror. '*Please*!'

'It's funny how Mr Brooks up and left without saying a word to anybody,' Mrs Graham said a few days later when she came in to give Crowell's room its weekly clean. 'Just like Mr Rogers who had the room before him. Both of 'em vanished without taking one stitch of their belongings other than what they stood up in!'

She stopped dusting suddenly and glanced down towards the floor. 'Oh, Mr Crowell, why didn't you tell me you upset that raspberry crumble I baked for you the other day? Look, there's a stain on the carpet!'

## THE QUIET MAN

*Terry Gisbourne*

Gibbet Terrace, Chingford, was never quite the same after that nasty business at No. 37. What veneer of suburban respectability it once had was now pitted and stained by the corrosive events which made the headlines in January 1936.

The *Daily Pictorial*, having voiced the nation's grief at the death of King George V, leapt back with characteristic vigour the next day, proclaiming 'Bloodbath in Gibbet Terrace – Family Victims of "Ritual Slaughter".' Later the case became known generally as 'The Animal Atrocities'. Some residents, anxious to preserve their lily-white reputations, left for cosier, more decent regions of Chingford. House values slumped. For many years those who stayed had to endure the intrusions of bizarre sightseers. But even today, some of the elderly living nearby can't help feeling a vestige of sympathy for their one-time neighbour at No. 35 who was hanged for the killings – quiet and dapper Jack Prince.

'Oh, Jack, I'm glad you're home.'

Violet Prince motioned her husband to come into the kitchen. Her sturdy build and ruddy complexion was proof that much of her life had been spent in the country. That evening, however, her friendly face had a brighter hue than usual.

'It's them next door again, Jack,' she whispered. 'I've been at my wits' end all afternoon. They haven't given me a minute's peace, banging on the walls and shouting. I'm afraid to think what they'll do next.'

Jack paused for an excuse but found it hard to hide his agitation.

'Perhaps they're moving some furniture about, having a spring clean. You know what some people are like, always shifting things around. Never satisfied with things the way they are.'

Violet gave him a knowing look.

'Let's not kid ourselves, love, We've been here for two months now and they've made trouble right from the start.'

Jack had never been one to make a scene. Like most retiring types he preferred the easy way out. But he had to admit that the Witlows were beginning to get on his nerves.

Jack Prince was a friendly, neat-looking northerner. Tidyness showed in his work and in the way he dressed. A creature of clean living but dominated by habit, some might say. He was tall and fairly well built, with brown eyes and short black hair parted so well you could see the white of his scalp. Jack was thirty-six and in eight years of marriage he and Violet had struggled to save enough to move south. They came from West Tadcaster, near Leeds, where Jack had kept a shop. The chance of buying bigger premises brought them to Chingford where Jack now had his shop in nearby Buchanan Street. Both were determined to get the business on its feet within a year. They planned to build a good customer relationship, to go through the books every night, and for Violet to help Jack out behind the counter four days a week. In the last few weeks their efforts were being rewarded. Trade was becoming more regular and customers quickly got to like their cheerful ways.

But Jack wished he could see some improvement in matters at home. The Witlows, it seemed, were bent on making their life a misery. At first the Princes had simply put the noise down to harmless high spirits. After two weeks, however, they were forced to the conclusion that the problem was more than just rowdy neighbours. Every evening when the Princes settled down in the lounge to some paperwork, the interruptions would start. A chorus of bangings and scrapings invariably gave way to what at first seemed like a row between the Witlows, only the astonished Princes learned later that the muffled verbal abuse was being directed at them. Then the bangings, like a poker being thrown against a grate, would resume with new intensity.

A month later the trouble increased. The Princes moved to other rooms to escape the noise, but this did not stop the Witlows. Somehow they would find out where the Princes were and proceed to create noise in whichever room was nearest. Faced with this impossible situation, Jack was now being forced to stay late at the shop some nights and finish his balancing there.

'What on earth can we do to reason with the bloody family?' Jack had once shouted in a rare moment of exasperation. Twice he had called next door to protest. On the first occasion he had simply got a blank 'don't know what you're talking about' response from Mrs Witlow, a squat, big-breasted woman with wide, staring eyes like a cow. She claimed her husband was out and wouldn't hear of such wild accusations, anyway. The second visit was even more negative – no one bothered to answer the door.

Despite Violet's requests, Jack flatly refused to call the police.

'Look at it this way, love,' he stressed. 'We've just got to consider the business. It won't be worth a ha'p'orth to us if we get tangled up in a court case. It'd be just like hanging dirty washing out in public. No, Vi, we've got to make the best of it for the time being, until the business is more on its feet, like. Then, who knows, we might be able to buy another house, a better place.'

'But for heaven's sake, Jack, aren't we going to do anything? We can't go on being treated like this. It'll get worse, I know it will.'

He tried reassuring her.

'There's no point getting worked up, Vi. We've got to stay

calm no matter what. If it'll make you feel any better, I've decided to go round again tonight and thrash this thing out once and for all. I'll make them see sense even if I have to . . . Well, they're going to get a piece of my mind, anyway.'

But Jack didn't dare tell her what he really thought. That talk and reason wouldn't stand a chance in hell. That the Witlows were a bunch of nutters who had it in for them. But why? Jack had thought long and hard about this and couldn't come up with any sane explanation. Mrs Witlow was the only member of the family he had seen, and that made it even more incredible. From talking to customers, he learned there were three in the family altogether – Mr and Mrs Witlow and a grown-up daughter named Audrey. Old man Witlow was a storeman at a local factory, while the daughter stayed at home all day with her mother. Jack had only seen Mrs Witlow to talk to just that once, but two or three times he had spotted her passing by his shop on the other side of the street. Perhaps he had seen the others before without realizing it. Perhaps they had even been to the shop. No, they wouldn't do that, he assured himself. In any case, he'd have noticed any strange-looking person like that, for they must look a bit insane to do what they've done, mustn't they?

What Violet couldn't appreciate was that they would have a very difficult job proving anything against the Witlows in court. They would deny everything, that was for sure. And any possibility of getting witnesses looked extremely remote. Jack had checked on the neighbours at No. 39 and found they were an old couple – as deaf as posts. Everyone he had spoken to described the Witlows as decent folk – 'good for a laugh, boisterous but well meaning.' So calling the law was out of the question, unless Jack was willing to risk the threat of losing the custom they had built up. And he just wasn't prepared to sacrifice that.

Initially, it was a silent confrontation on the Witlows' doorstep. The two of them stood there weighing each other up. Jack had this awkward feeling that he was the pursued finally facing the pursuer. Mr Witlow simply glared insolently as if to say, 'Right, we'll have a bit of fun with the bugger.'

He was a burly, balding brick of a man, a little shorter than Jack but wider. His big belly swelled out over the leather belt which held up his soiled corduroys. Jack noted the small eyes, the pinky pigmentation of his hairless skin, and half expected

Mr Witlow to let out a snort rather than say, 'Clear off'. He had one hand on the half-open door as if he was about to bang it shut in Jack's face. Jack gave a little nervous cough, but his voice was calm and possessed authority.

'Well, Mr Witlow, I don't have to tell you why I have called, do I . . . ?'

Before he could finish what he had to say, Mr Witlow bawled for 'Else', his wife, to come to the door. Jack, a bit taken aback by the vehemence of the interruption, began to falter.

'I'm asking you to pack it in, stop this stupid troublemaking. It won't get you anywhere.'

By this time Else and her daughter Audrey, a long-necked girl with a prominent nose, were at the door.

Mr Witlow sucked on his teeth. The glint in his eyes was beginning to irritate Jack. 'Else, is this the bloke who troubled you that time? Came making all kinds of accusations and insinuations? This him?'

She nodded. 'Yes, that's him.'

'Well then, mister, you'd be best off making yourself scarce. If there's one thing I can't stand it's bloody busybodies making a nuisance of themselves.'

Jack butted in. 'Look here, hold on a minute. Let's get this straight. I've a damn good right to be a nuisance as you call it after what we've had to put up with from you lot. What have you got against us, tell me that? Where's the sense? If you can't see reason, at least give me an explanation.'

Too late, Jack realized that he had slipped up. He hadn't meant to get excited, but they had cunningly succeeded in baiting him. His plan had been to play it calm and cool and not get too emotional.

'Do you know what he's talking about Else, because I'm blowed if I do. I'd say he's got a screw loose.'

Else, her arms folded across her wide bosom, looked upwards mournfully and tossed her head in bovine fashion. 'Don't know what the world's coming to when it can't take care of nosey-parkers. Ought to be locked up.'

Jack gave a gasp of disgust. 'Well, that's a laugh and no mistake. Anyway, let's not beat about the bush. You've had your bit of fun. Now try to be rational and see our side of it. How would you like it if we were to play hell every night you came home. You'd want some peace and quiet the same as any other person. It's not much to ask.'

Was it Jack's imagination or did the arrogant gleam in Mr Witlow's eyes suddenly become brighter? He turned and grinned at his wife, then relaxed his hold on the door. 'Seeing how you put it that way . . . what's it worth?'

Jack paused. 'I don't understand . . . What do you mean by "what's it worth"?'

'What I say.' Mr Witlow proceeded to measure his words carefully. 'You're a man of means . . . a man of property . . . Got a shop, haven't you? Now we might, and I say might, just show a little consideration to you and your wife . . . for a little consideration in return. But if you can't see your way to, how shall we say, obliging us, then we might just let it slip among the folk round here that we have to put up with terrible goings-on next door.' Mr Witlow beamed. 'How's trade, then? Not too slack I hope.'

Jack managed to look calm, but underneath he was boiling with anger. So that was their game, A blatant piece of nasty, sordid, old-fashioned blackmail. Oh yes, he got the picture all right. A bit of free stuff from the shop in return for a little peace and quiet. Not complete peace and quiet, you understand, but just a little. Jack struggled to control his wild, pent-up emotions. For two pins he would belt Witlow and tell him what to do with his foul suggestions. But no, that wouldn't be playing their game, would it? Cunning needed to be matched with cunning. He also needed time to think. So for now he would play along with the Witlows. Make them think they had him licked. A little humility was called for. 'Well yes, Mr Witlow . . . I take your point. I've no doubts that I can arrange something. Say tomorrow night? I could drop something by on the way home.'

A smug smile of satisfaction settled on Mr Witlow's face. 'Now he's talking, eh, Else? I knew he'd come round to our way of thinking.'

Jack returned home nursing alien feelings of extreme unpleasantness. His right hand was shaking as he turned the key in the lock. If they thought they could do this to Jack Prince and get away with it . . . Who did they take him for? A country yokel who didn't know better? A half-baked northerner out of his depth? He was sure of one thing – that Violet would never be told of the 'arrangement' with the Witlows. She at least would be spared the pain of being forced to bargain with them. Less than an hour ago he would have laughed at any mention of 'peace at a price'.

His thoughts were interrupted by Violet's voice coming from the front room 'Quick, Jack, is that you?'

He turned round and she ran into the hall.

'They're at it again, Jack, making horrible noises.'

Jack strode past her into the room and was greeted by a cacophonous assault on the eardrums. The wall by the fireplace sounded as if it was being rubbed and scored with rough sandpaper. In the corner near the writing bureau came the tap, tap of something striking cold metal. But, despite this confusion of sound, Jack's hearing was also aware of a new and even more ghastly din. The rhythm and pitch came unmistakably from human voices chanting.

'Oink, oink, oink . . . moo, moo, moo . . . quack, quack, quack . . . oink, oink, oink . . .' And so it went on. Jack turned to Violet in exasperation.

'I don't believe it . . . I just don't believe it.'

Two weeks passed and the Witlows' troublemaking continued, but to a lesser degree. Jack, true to his word, had twice called on the family with 'peace offerings' and they, surprisingly, had responded by cutting down on the noise.

They seemed content at present just to hammer away on the wall for about twenty minutes every evening. But that was followed by the new, bizarre display of animal noises. The grunts and snorts and similar farmyard impressions always lasted for exactly ten minutes, and then sweet silence would reign again.

Violet, however, lived in dread of the ritual. Whenever the Witlows started, she would retreat to the kitchen to be out of earshot. It wasn't just the noise, she told Jack, but a feeling at the back of her mind that it meant something evil.

The whole business was also having a big effect on Jack, but he would never admit to it. That was his trouble. He would simply say they were a damned nuisance, and that they'd soon get tired of it. He didn't mention the sleepless nights he was having, the 'arrangement' he'd struck with the Witlows, the dark thoughts he was entertaining. Violet had noticed that Jack wasn't his even-tempered self. He was nervy, irritable, inclined to argue on small matters which normally would have been dismissed lightly. She wasn't to know that Jack had entered the critical stage of a nervous condition. His resistance to stress had sunk to a low ebb. Bottled-up feelings were fighting for possession of his mind.

Even Jack wasn't aware of the dangerous undercurrents. The only warning appeared to be occasional bouts of headache, but these he put down to overwork. It was true he had put in more time at the shop, mainly to take his mind off the business at home. But he found it exceedingly hard to concentrate, and invariably his thoughts lingered on the knotty problem of the Witlows.

Paradoxically, Jack's nervous state was brought about by himself. He was completely unable to feel anything but absolute loathing for the family. Had he joked or even remarked about the idiot antics to one of his regular customers, the intensity of bad feeling may have subsided. But to Jack this wasn't a matter to be talked about. His mind had now told him that it was a very personal insult, something so offensive he wouldn't even discuss it properly with Violet. And so the rot within was nibbling slowly but inexorably away at brittle, taut nerves. It needed just a little more aggravation to accelerate the process.

He was walking down a narrow, winding country lane. The stillness of that hot summer's day was broken only by the sounds of bees searching for pollen in the hedgerows. There wasn't even a wisp of breeze to temper the golden warmth that bathed meadow and valley. And this is how Jack liked it. He was completely at peace with the world. Everyone, it seemed, had been lulled to sleep by the sheer tranquillity of warm, unspoilt, undisturbed open space. No one to bother you. Just left to dream of rural havens like this, far away from the confined, noisy hustle and bustle of town.

Then a noise intruded on his thoughts and he looked up. There was nothing in sight, but the sound was unmistakably that of a pig. The grunts and snorts continued at such a rate that it seemed as if the poor animal was in distress. It must be round the next corner in the lane. And the farther Jack walked, the louder the noise became. Thinking it may have injured itself, he increased his step and rounded the bend. The sight which greeted his eyes froze him to the spot. For there, standing in the middle of the lane was not only a pig but also a cow and a duck. His appearance prompted a burst of noise from all of them. To Jack it appeared that they were chanting at him, but what he couldn't believe as he stared at them was that each one looked like one of the Witlows.

Elsie Witlow's face could be seen in the cow as it tossed its head in apparent contempt. There was Audrey Witlow, wings flapping wildly and feathers bristling. And who could mistake old man Witlow as he snorted and screamed on all fours? They advanced towards him and their chant became louder. Jack stumbled backwards, still not able to believe it. No amount of blinking and rubbing of eyes could remove the frightening sight.

He turned and retreated, but as he did so they came after him. He broke into a run with them in hot pursuit. The snorts, mooings and quacks were barely a yard behind. But the horror of it all was that he couldn't shake them off. No matter how fast he ran, the noises were always a few feet away and getting louder all the time. Sweat was pouring down Jack's terrified face as he gasped and panted. They were getting closer and he couldn't do a thing about it. His lungs felt as though they were about to burst. Mist was forming over his eyes. He had to give up. 'Can't go on . . . can't go on . . . can't go . . .'

Jack lay in darkness, trying to get his breath back. Blurred shapes seemed vaguely familiar to him. He struggled to raise himself and his eyes caught sight of the dressing-table next to him. Giving a low groan he lay back on the bed. It had all been a horrible nightmare . . . But had it?

Jack listened. He could still hear the noises. The chant seemed more distant yet strangely near to hand. He stared upwards. But no, it couldn't be . . . the sounds were definitely coming from above . . . from the loft. He heard something shuffling and then a noise like plaster being kicked on to the loft floor. That confirmed Jack's suspicions.

'The bastards . . . the bloody . . .'

The door of the bedroom opened and Violet switched on the light. She was holding a bottle of tablets and a glass of water. Her voice trembled.

'Are you all right, Jack? This'll make you feel better. For heaven's sake, what are we going to do?'

A little over a day later, there was a knock at the Witlows' front door. It was just after ten o'clock.

Every Monday morning, Florrie Hebditch called on Elsie Witlow for a cup of tea and a natter. It was a little custom of theirs. Mrs Witlow would pop round to Mrs Hebditch one Monday and vice versa the next Monday and so on. If one of them had to go shopping, the other would have a key to let themselves in and wait.

Mrs Hebditch pulled a face. There was no reply. This was the second time running Elsie had gone out and, besides, Florrie was dying to tell her a bit of gossip she couldn't have heard. Mr Brown, from Summerland Terrace, had gone and left his wife for a gypsy woman that very morning.

'Came right out of the blue, Elsie. Talking to Mrs Travers, I was. Then who should come storming out of No. 23 but Mr Brown with a suitcase. "I'm going," he says, "and I'm not coming back." Yelling at her from the gate. She just shouts something I wouldn't repeat and throws a couple of cups and saucers after him. Then she spots me across the street. Honestly, Elsie, if looks could have killed . . .' Mrs Hebditch had the tale off pat. She had never liked Mrs Brown and her stuck-up ways, anyway.

Using the key from her handbag, Mrs Hebditch fiddled with the lock and opened the front door.

*Drip . . .*

It opened into a black-and-white tiled hall that swept past the stairs and into the kitchen.

*Drip . . .*

Where could that woman have got to? Mrs Hebditch frowned and shut the door behind her.

*Drip . . .*

Well, a nice cup of tea won't go amiss. Elsie will be ready for one.

*Drip . . .*

What's that dripping noise? Must be one of the taps.

*Drip . . .*

Mrs Hebditch turned round in the hall and her mouth sagged wide open. Red swamped her vision. The passageway was bathed in it, the walls and stairs splashed, streaked, daubed and dotted with it. She stepped forward blindly and felt her feet slipping on the stuff.

'Elsie . . .' She gave an involuntary cry.

Can't be paint . . . didn't tell me they were decorating . . . oh, my God. Mrs Hebditch began to panic and shiver. Then her eyes caught sight of red blobs dripping into the pool by the stairs. Instinctively, she raised her head slowly upwards, even though something was telling her not to. She wished she hadn't.

That afternoon there were quite a few comings and goings

at Chingford police station. News of the Witlow killings had shaken the local constabulary out of their lethargy and produced a burst of activity, the likes of which had never before been witnessed. A passer-by had raised the alarm after finding Mrs Hebditch in a collapsed state on the Witlows' doorstep. Chingford police, faced with a massacre, decided it was a job for Scotland Yard. And the Yard, after a cursory examination of the gruesome findings, surmised with unusual haste that it could be a ritual slaughter linked with witchcraft.

But while detectives sifted the evidence at No. 37, a major if less colourful event was taking place at the police station. Amid all the excitement, no one noticed the dapper, passive-looking man waiting at the station counter. He kept looking from one officer to another, trying to attract their attention.

'Excuse me,' he called. One of the officers turned round.

'Oh, I'm sorry, sir. Bit of a panic going on. What can I do for you?'

'My name's Jack Prince. I'd like to see someone about the business at 37, Gibbet Terrace.'

Detective-Inspector Robert Sanders sat down at the desk facing Jack Prince. He was absent-mindedly fingering a pencil. 'Now, tell me why you think you killed the Witlow family.'

The undertone of sarcasm in the officer's voice was deliberate. Damn it, he was busy. He had a meeting with the forensic boys in an hour's time, and the Commissioner was breathing down his neck for a progress report on the case that evening.

It was equally irritating to him that he couldn't unload this customer on to one of his men because they were working on more important aspects of the case. Cranks were a thorn in the thumb to Detective-Inspector Sanders, and he feared he was looking at one now.

'I'm waiting, Mr Prince,' he snapped impatiently. Jack looked up in surprise.

'What . . . ? Oh yes, I'm sorry. I have a job to concentrate just lately.' He moved restlessly in the chair. 'Well, I'd just had as much as I could stand from them. They were our neighbours, you see. Noisy lot right from the start. Driving the wife out of her mind they were. So I put paid to their little games for good.'

'And how exactly did you put paid to their little games?' said the detective, still refusing to believe the tale.

'I stayed up Sunday night and waited for them to go to bed. Vi had taken something to make her sleep. I must have waited until about three on the Monday morning, and then I decided the time had come. I'd even sharpened my knife for the job.

'I climbed over the back garden fence and got in through a kitchen window they had left open. The stairs squeaked a bit but it didn't worry me. I could still hear snoring coming from the bedrooms. I made a quick guess that the back bedroom was Audrey Witlow's because it was the smallest. So I settled for her first. I didn't mess about. I crept in and switched on the light just in time to see her turning over. I struck once, severing her jugular.'

Detective-Inspector Sanders stopped playing with the pencil. His pulse was starting to race. He leaned forward gently. 'What happened next?'

'Well, I came back out of the bedroom on to the landing. I went to open the front bedroom door. I had my hand on the handle and felt it turning. The next thing who should I come face to face with but old man Witlow standing there in his pyjamas, staring at me as if he was seeing things. I didn't have much time to play with, so his heart got my knife, all ten inches of it. Don't worry, he didn't suffer. I don't make mistakes like that.

'There was still Mrs Witlow, of course. I switched on the light and she was just getting out of bed. She screamed but it didn't last long. I cut her off in mid-stream, again slashing the jugular.' Jack sighed. 'That was it . . . I'd done it. But I wasn't finished yet.' He gave a chuckle. 'I'd brought some meat hooks and twine with me. I lashed their feet together and hung them side by side from the landing. Then I took my knife and ripped their stomachs open. Oh, it was a mess, all right.

'It's a bit of a laugh now when I think about it, but it was just what they deserved. Kind of fitting, I thought. You see they were pigs . . . animals . . . didn't know any different. They needed to be slaughtered like pigs.

'I almost forgot about the knife. You'll find it on the table in my shop . . . the butcher's in Buchanan Street.'

# A WALK ALONG THE BEACH

*Frances Stephens*

The car nosed its way along the single-track road by the coast, where bleak moorland stretched down to a stony beach. Ahead lay the cliffs of Dirk Point. The sea looked sullen and grey.

Judith Scott shivered, glancing surreptitiously at her husband, Gordon was still angry. His chin jutted obstinately, and his hands were rigid on the driving wheel. The trouble was, he couldn't stomach the child.

'Little monster,' Gordon had called him. 'Revolting little freak.'

In the back seat, a four-year-old boy sat nursing a tiny dog. His chubby fingers wound artlessly into the woolly fur, pinching and squeezing, so that the creature squealed and scrabbled with its miniature paws. But the boy held on. The excitement in his eyes belied the childish innocence of his face.

The car bumped over a pot-hole, and pink lips curved in a smile as the fingers dug deeper. The dog started a mounting whine that set Judith's teeth on edge. She turned around.

'Tod. Give the dog to me.'

'No.'

'Come along now. Give me the dog.'

'Snowy is *my* dog. Mummy bought him for me to play with.'

Firmly, Judith stretched out a hand, but the child shrank back, rebellion in every line of his body.

'Leave me alone. I won't – I won't – '

In exasperation, Gordon Scott ran the car on to a grassy patch by the roadside and jammed on the brake. It was humiliating to be beaten by a four-year-old child, but Judith tried to make her voice cheerful.

'A bit of fresh air is what we need. A walk along the beach.'

Recklessly, the dog darted towards a patch of rough weeds, and freedom, whilst the boy headed for the stretches of mud and pebbles.

'Let them go,' said Gordon, 'God knows, we've earned a rest.'

The sea was well out, the beach and road were deserted, so

little harm could come to the child. Judith sighed as she watched him pick his way purposefully in the direction of a clump of rocks. There was something almost repellent about the squat figure with its air of determination.

Moodily, Gordon lit a cigarette.

'Trust us to get lumbered with that little horror again. The way he treats that dog makes me want to throw up.'

Judith smiled faintly.

'His mother says he loves animals.'

'Loves animals?' Gordon's tone was savage. 'Snaring birds to poke their eyes out, tearing the wings off living butterflies . . .'

'But she says it shows scientific interest – that he'll probably become a vet.'

Her voice was almost pleading, as though she wanted Gordon's reassurance that this could be so. But her husband was silent. They were both oppressed by the presence of this child who had been thrust on them through no fault of their own.

A week ago, Judith and Gordon had arrived in search of a quiet holiday. Married for ten years, a childless couple, they had slipped into an easy, companionable relationship. Solitude suited them, and Dirk Point, within easy driving distance, was one of the most desolate regions they could find.

Their hotel was fully booked. Among the guests was Mrs Hunter, a garrulous woman, petulantly pretty, looks already fading. Assiduously searching for any listener, she poured out the most intimate details of her personal life. Gordon dismissed her as a professional moaner, drifting from place to place.

The woman's husband had obviously seen the warning light and divorced her, although making ample provision for his wife and child. She doted on the boy.

'Isn't he a precious darling?' cooed Mrs Hunter, and Judith felt faintly sick at the sugar in her voice.

'He was such a darling toddler. Tod. I still call him Tod.'

Disgusted at the empty-headed woman and her spoilt brat, Gordon had tried to steer clear.

'Avoid them,' he said curtly.

But it had not been possible. Four days before, Mrs Hunter, after being taken violently ill, had been removed to hospital for an emergency operation. That left Tod. There were no relations to call upon. No one.

As a temporary measure, other guests had offered to help

out by taking turns at looking after the boy. But, curiously, after initial contact their enthusiasm evaporated. Today it had fallen to the Scotts – again.

Gordon swung his long legs out of the car.

'Are you coming?'

His voice was still irritable. Judith narrowed her eyes, gazing along the uninviting shingle.

'Perhaps we shouldn't let him go too far away.'

'He can't go far enough for me. Something about that kid makes my flesh crawl.'

The stones hurt her feet, biting through the thin soles of her sandals as she hurried to keep up with Gordon. The beach panned out as they edged their way along by horizontal slabs of rock, treacherous with dark slime. Here were pools of stagnant water never reached by the sun. The air was tainted. Not the rich ripeness of seaweed, more the rank odour of some other rot and decay.

'What a disgusting place this is.' Scowling, Gordon sent a pebble skimming across the ground. As gravel spattered, Judith's eyes were drawn downward to a blob of yellowish jelly only inches from her feet. Frayed strands, blood red, threaded the opaque body in an obscene mapwork. Moulded over the pebbles, the creature resembled an oozing nightmare. It was the biggest jellyfish she had ever seen.

Judith tugged at Gordon's sleeve, indicating her find with a nervous gesture.

'That's not the first,' he said. 'They're all over the place.'

Judith tucked her arm in his. Alerted now, their eyes scanned the ground as they picked their way forward. Nestling evilly in the crevices of rocks, sprawling on the shingle, flabby and totally repellent, there were jellyfish everywhere.

One rippled like an oily parasite over a remnant of bleached driftwood. Others, semi-liquid and vile, nestled in the straggling vegetation.

Judith's hand tightened on Gordon's arm, as fearfully they peered into a deep cleft filled with water. Stranded by the tide, a fringed jellyfish drifted, like some relic from the dawn of time. Febrile tentacles wafted with the ripples. The body was bleary, almost bloated.

'They're like no species I've ever seen,' said Gordon. 'It's as though they've developed in some gross and abnormal way, as though . . .'

Judith flinched as a flurry of barking filled the air.

'The kid,' she gasped. 'We should never have let them wander off.'

Twenty yards away, along the beach, the excited animal was snapping at something on the ground. Emitting short, staccato barks, it would jerk forward with its quivering nose, then leap on stiff legs, as though in a transport of delirium. The dog was wild with a mixture of fear and intoxication, as it bit and bit again.

It was Gordon who first saw Tod. Somewhere he had discovered a length of rusty piping, which he brandished as he ran, plunging viciously at the jellyfish, prodding them, poking them, red-faced from his exertion, grunting and squealing with satisfaction. His object was destruction. Every inch of him spelled out an orgy of hate.

Judith swallowed the bile that rose in her throat, for some of the jellyfish were bleeding a thick milky fluid. The stench of it was on her lips.

'Stop that!'

Gordon's voice cracked like a whip. Tod paused for a moment, in the act of striking, then sent the rod clattering on to the ground. A moment later, he was gathering up pebbles and heaving them at the middles of the jellyfish.

'I said stop it!'

'Hear them hiss. Listen, listen.'

The boy's face was suffused with a feverish colour, his hands had more than childlike strength as he lobbed stone after stone.

'The sharp ones are best.'

Goaded beyond endurance, Gordon grabbed the boy's shoulders, shaking him until the stone fell out of his tightly-clenched hand.

'Leave me alone. Leave me alone!'

Tod's voice rose to a crescendo of stormy weeping. His face set in grim lines of distaste as Gordon kept his grip on the child. Gradually the sobs died down. Tod raised his face. The small eyes were puffy. They gleamed with malevolence.

'I hate you.'

'Do you now? It's time to go.'

'Where's Snowy? You didn't stop *him*. Where's Snowy?'

Hypnotized by the wild tantrum she had just witnessed, Judith had forgotten the dog. Now all three of them stared around. Afternoon was turning the sky to streaks of sulphur yellow. The sea looked alien, and the tide was on the turn. A gull screeched over the empty beach.

'Go back to the car and wait.'

There was something in Gordon's voice that told Judith it would be dangerous to disobey. Stifling her repugnance, she seized Tod's hand and set off purposefully along the sand. The hand in hers was wet and clammy. Resolutely, Judith's fingers tightened.

Half an hour dragged by. Through the car window, Judith could see the figure of her husband, pacing this way and that, calling, searching. Tod sat in sulky silence. A mutter of words would rise to his lips, and he would thresh his legs violently, then subside into a smouldering bundle of resentment.

Gordon returned to the car. His face had such a closed look that Judith left her questions unasked. The silence grew and grew. Even the child was uneasy. As Gordon lit a cigarette, Judith felt a throb of dismay, for her husband's hands were unsteady.

'One more look,' said Gordon. 'One more, and then we must go.'

The dog was still missing when they left, and the waves were creeping over the beach. Tod had fallen asleep.

Judith settled back. The car skimmed along the road by the moors, where the shadows of darkness were already gathering. Distant against the skyline, they passed the glass and concrete of the nuclear power station, with its cooling towers and grey-green dome. Judith thought wretchedly of the lost dog.

Tired and depressed, she decided on an early night, leaving Gordon to masculine company in the bar downstairs. She had scarcely had time to relax when a sudden burst of anguished screaming set every nerve jangling. Doors opened, people hurried backwards and forwards, as Tod howled like a soul in torment. Judith tried to shut out the sound. The noise continued.

By and by came a tentative tap on the door. Sighing, Judith pulled on a housecoat and faced the hotel manager, harassed by unwelcome responsibilities.

'If you'd come for a few moments, Mrs Scott – just a few moments. He keeps saying something about going to the beach . . .'

It was midnight when Gordon came upstairs, and Judith was still wide awake. Her husband had evaded all the commotion, but she could scarcely blame him for that. He listened as she told him of the promise she had made to Tod, to take him back to the beach. The price of silence.

'It isn't the dog he cares about. You know that?' Gordon was looking at her intently. 'He has his own twisted reasons for going back. He's forgotten that poor little beast by now.'

Pulling back the blankets, Gordon prepared to get into bed, but Judith could tell he had something else to say. She waited as her husband lay staring into the darkness, his hands behind his head.

'I was talking to a man in the bar. Local character. Knows this coast blindfold.'

A pause.

'I told him about the beach with the jellyfish. People round here never go there.'

'But why?' Judith's voice was a whisper.

'Two years ago, there was a panic at the nuclear power station. It was all hushed up. There would have been mass hysteria otherwise.'

Judith's face was taut with strain.

'There was leakage of radio-active waste. The locals swear that it affected natural life, causing gross development and deformity.'

'Like . . .'

'Like the jellyfish we saw this afternoon.'

Judith reached for his hand.

'I never want to go to that place again.'

'Don't worry,' said Gordon firmly. 'After tomorrow, you never will.'

Tod was ready and waiting. He hopped impatiently from foot to foot. With some misgivings, Judith saw that the boy had brought a spade. Only this was not the usual childish toy. The shaft was massive, and the blade was keen and cruel.

There were no other cars on the road around the coast. Again, Gordon parked on the patch of grass. The sea was a long way out.

Almost bursting with eagerness, Tod pulled at the door handle, gibbering with pleasure as he tumbled out. A froth of saliva covered his lips. His face was lit from inside.

Judith watched him go shouting down the beach, brandishing the spade. Gordon sat back. The place filled Judith with nausea. It was hateful, inimical. But she still had a certain responsibility towards the child.

'I'd better go with him.'

Gordon laid a hand on her arm.

'There's no hurry. Stay a while.'

As the minutes dragged by, Judith thought of the travesty this holiday had turned out to be. A child – somehow it all hinged on this diabolical child.

'I don't expect he'll find the dog.'

The certainty in her own voice surprised her.

'No.'

Gordon's answer was clipped, almost flippant.

'I didn't tell you everything I heard in the bar last night.'

Sick at heart, Judith knew that she did not want to hear. But that she must.

'There's a whisper that the jellyfish have depraved appetites. That they feed on flesh – animal and human flesh – and that they have a highly-developed instinct for finding it.'

Eyes wide with horror, Judith searched her husband's face.

'You *never* believe . . .'

'I don't know,' answered Gordon slowly. 'But yesterday, when I was looking for the dog, I saw its collar in a pool of mucus – as though it had been regurgitated. And there were bloody tufts of fur.'

Judith remembered the way her husband had gone back – to make sure.

A thousand devils of doubt and disbelief were hammering in her brain. Shock drenched her.

'Tod!'

'Wait a minute.'

Gordon's grip was vice-like.

'Imagine that little monster – cutting – mutilating – bubbling with sadistic pleasure. Think of him five years from now, ten, proceeding from one atrocity to another. A boy who never was a child . . .'

This was a nightmare. Judith tried to recover some remnants of sanity and calm. Even admitting that Tod's character had been rotted and eroded, so that he found childish pleasures too tame, Gordon was going too far.

'This is unthinkable,' she said shakily. 'A jellyfish couldn' attack a child. Not one jellyfish. Not ten.'

'There were hundreds,' said Gordon laconically.

'How can you sit there?' Judith raised a trembling hand to her face.

'Why not? Who'd ever believe a load of highly-coloured rubbish like that?'

Pulling her glance away from her husband's inscrutable expression, Judith looked towards the beach. Then she was out on the shingle, running, gasping, as the stones cut her feet.

Panic made her careless. Judith sobbed for breath as the ground hissed and squelched beneath her feet. There were jellyfish everywhere.

'Tod! Tod!'

An edge of rock gashed her leg, making her wince and bend, raising a hand that was sticky with the warm smell of blood. Mortal fear possessed her. On she stumbled, lungs bursting, eyes devouring the empty shore.

Discarded lay an empty sandal. Ten yards away, a spade.

'Tod! Tod!'

No answer. Back in the car, Gordon smiled.

## THE CATOMADO

*R. Chetwynd-Hayes*

Martin tried to throw Myna out of the window but she would not go.

'Stop messing about,' she complained, while her head dangled over the window-sill and her really hideous legs became entangled with the curtains. 'You know I don't like horseplay.'

There was nothing he could do but pull her back and mutter bad-temperedly, 'Spoil-sport.'

Myna patted her thatch of black hair, which looked like a dirty mop. 'Honestly, you're like a schoolboy with an obsession for heights. I'll never forget that day when you made me pose for a photograph on the top of a high cliff. "Take a step back," you said. "Just one more step." There could have been a nasty accident. Think of how you would have felt then.'

Martin thought of insurance policies, the house she owned, money – all manner of mundane and boring things – then groaned.

'Exactly.' Myna nodded and her awful hair flopped over her low forehead. 'You would have never forgiven yourself.'

'I've got a very forgiving nature,' Martin muttered as he watched her trot off to the kitchen, where she would doubtlessly fry some more sausages.

Myna had a thing about sausages. She liked to fry them on one side only, so they burst and all the grease-oozing filling erupted like an over-ripe boil. Sausages cannot be accepted as a motive for murder, but when cooked in a certain way, and dished up as a steady diet over a long period, they can become an important ingredient. Her voice called from the kitchen.

'Din-dins ready!'

Like a dog summoned to meat, Martin went forth to his split sausages and burnt chips.

He who seeks, finds. After five days of searching, Martin found his perfect wife-disposal unit. It was a disused lighthouse set a hundred yards inland on the south coast, and some enterprising scrap-metal merchant had removed the iron railings from the top platform. Martin looked down at the three-hundred-foot drop to the road below and wondered why there wasn't a sign stating: BRING UNWANTED WIVES HERE. It was a wife-murderer's dream. A parricidal Mecca. A perfect aid to instant divorce. Martin rubbed his hands, then allegorically girded his loins for action.

Myna hated climbing stairs. She was also inclined to be a little inquisitive.

'Why,' she demanded, 'must we climb three hundred steps to look at the sea?'

Martin was rather at a loss for a feasible explanation, but he found one.

'On a clear day you can see the coast of France.'

Myna was irritatingly practical. 'But it's foggy.'

Martin's sense of well-being made him a little careless. 'Yes. No one will see a thing.'

'There you are, then.' Myna's face had turned to an interesting shade of purple and Martin wondered if she might not have a heart attack and save him a lot of trouble. 'What's the point of climbing a lot of stairs when we won't see a thing?'

Martin became desperate. 'The downward view is quite breath-taking.'

With great reluctance she continued her upward trudge. Suddenly she stopped.

'Let's get one thing clear. I'm not posing for any photographs.'

'I haven't brought a camera.'

'That's all right, then.'

When they came out on to the narrow platform, Myna was panting like an overworked steam-engine, though, to Martin's disgust, she soon recovered. Fog banks were rolling in from the sea, but there was visibility for about ten feet. Myna was mildly appreciative.

'Not a bad view. A bit whirly and misty, but not bad. Not worth the trouble of climbing all this way, though.'

'You must look down,' Martin instructed. 'You can see a long way down.'

Myna obligingly edged her way to the rim of the platform and looked down.

'Yes, you're right. I can see the ground quite clearly. Oh, look, there's our car. Isn't it small?'

'I should move a few steps to the right,' Martin advised. He did not want her falling on top of the car – it had been resprayed only last week. 'If you look right, you'll see where the road meets the pavement.'

Myna bent forward and presented her broad rump for Martin's consideration.

'I can't see it.'

'You soon will.'

Martin raised his foot, gently laid the sole of his shoe against the generously-rounded contours, and pushed.

It would be nice to record that Myna flew like a bird. But she didn't. She fell like a fat woman who has been kicked off a tall building. She went straight down, arms flailing, legs kicking, and landed, after a swift journey of some three hundred feet, with a most satisfactory – if somewhat sickening – thud. Martin was quite pleased.

He did a little dance, then made for the stairs.

He ran down twelve, then stopped to rehearse his lines.

'I tried to stop her, but she would go . . . Oh, no, I stayed by the car . . . If I could get my hands on the man who removed them railings . . . I would strangle him.' Jolly good.

He skipped down another hundred steps singing an impromptu ditty.

'No more bangers,
Lots of lovely lolly,
She went down with lots of clangers,
Because she had no brolly.'

When he had descended some two hundred steps, he met Myna coming up. She was rather breathless and more than a little flustered. She sat down on a step and mopped a moist brow on the sleeve of her dress.

'There you are. Strewth, that gave me a nasty turn!'

Martin did not speak. He gave a brilliant performance of a man who has discarded speech and wishes to communicate by bulging eyes and gaping mouth. Myna noted his expression.

'What's the matter with you, then? You sickening for something?'

Martin shook his head.

'That's all right, then. Oh, me stomach was in me mouth when I fell like that. I hit the pavement with quite a wallop, you know. I expect you can't forgive yourself for taking me up there.'

Martin shook his head again. This time most vigorously. Myna got up. 'Well, it's no use crying over spilt milk. Let's go home and I'll fry you some nice sausages. All squelchy, the way you like 'em.'

Martin sucked an indigestion tablet and tried to remember – if indeed he had ever known – how fast a body would be travelling at the end of a three-hundred-foot drop. He decided to allow three feet per second and, assisted by his fingers and a sheet of paper, came to the conclusion that Myna had hit the pavement at something like fifty miles an hour.

'She ought to have been a bag of jelly,' he muttered.

Myna herself refused to discuss the matter.

'Can't you forget this obsession for heights? All you seem to think about is high places and people falling. You might consider my feelings. It was an unpleasant experience.'

'But – ' Martin insisted.

'Not another word. Have some fat over your bangers.'

'I guess you could boil anything in that,' the old man in the junk shop stated.

'It's heavy,' Martin agreed.

They stood looking at the iron stockpot with silent admiration. It was indeed a formidable vessel; measuring three feet across and two deep, it was constructed from solid cast-iron. Martin's eyes glittered and he could scarcely ask the next question.

'How heavy would you say it was?'

The old man pursed his lips, then sighed as though he were parting with a state secret.

'Tidy weight, sir. If you were to press me, sir, I'd say fifty-six pound if it's an ounce. Wouldn't care to drop it on me foot, sir, and that's a fact.'

Martin grinned like a wolf who has spotted Red Riding-Hood. 'Or head.'

The old man thought that remark to be the epitome of outrageous humour. He crackled, then coughed, before wiping his eyes on a piece of old curtain.

'You're a coughdrop, sir. On yer head! If that iron pot was to drop on yer head, sir, it would crack it, sir – crack it like a rotten egg – and there'd be nothing left, sir, but an 'orrible mess of splintered bones, sir, and spilt brains.'

Martin reached for his wallet.

'How much?'

The old man looked thoughtful.

'I could say four pounds, sir, and then I'd be giving it away. But seeing you're a gentleman who'll give it a good home, and put it – I've no manner of doubt – to good use, let's say two nicker and no argument.'

Martin handed over two one-pound notes, then took up his purchase and staggered to the door.

Myna was not overjoyed.

'You can't fry sausages in that.'

'But you could boil them,' Martin hastened to point out, then added wistfully: 'It would be a change.'

Myna brightened at this prospect. 'That's an idea, but don't you think it's a bit big?'

'I'd say just the right size.'

She shrugged. 'If you say so. But you'll have to lift it for me.'

He decided the best place where Myna could obtain the fullest fortuitous effect from a falling stockpot would be in the hall – three flights down. If he stood on the landing and held the pot over the banisters, then dropped it when Myna stepped on to the third black tile from the right, it should hit her square on. He had a dummy run.

She came upstairs carrying an enamel basin.

'You ought to be more careful. This hit me head.'

He assumed an expression of deep concern.

'Sorry. It slipped out of my hand. Did it hurt you?'

'No. But the enamel's chipped.'

Next day he went for the real thing. Myna took up her shopping bag, put on her awful hat that needed two long pins to keep it in position, then prepared to depart.

'Shan't be long.'

'Take care,' he said.

She seemed to take ages to descend three flights of stairs, and his arms ached from the effort required to hold a fifty-six-pound stockpot over the target area. Then she stepped out on to that tiled floor and Martin released his bomb.

It went down, straight and true. A black, bulbous vessel, with its handle standing out to one side like a stiff tail. It crashed down on to that awful hat with a clanging thud and Martin almost fell over the banisters with excitement. He went back into the flat to compose his new lines.

'Was carrying pot along landing to kitchen . . . it slipped . . . went over banisters . . . never forgive myself . . .' Now I'd better get downstairs and start yelling my head off.

He heard footsteps coming up the stairs. Heavy, slow treads, and he dismissed an incredible suspicion as downright ridiculous. He waited. The footsteps came up on to the landing and stopped, then the door opened and Myna entered, hugging the stockpot to her more-than-capacious bosom. The steep climb, plus the weight of the stockpot, had made her more breathless than usual.

'I told you . . . I told you . . . Don't be so careless. This thing ruined me 'at.'

Martin fainted.

Myna put brown paper soaked in vinegar on Martin's forehead, and held a burnt feather under his nose. The combination had the desired effect. He returned to full consciousness and rather wished he had not. There was the stockpot sitting smugly on the floor, and there was Myna ruefully examining her ruined hat.

'Feeling better, ducks?' she inquired.

He said, 'Yes,' and tried to understand why and how. There appeared to be no rational explanation.

'You . . .' he hesitated. 'How do you feel?'

She smiled cheerfully. 'Me? I'm fine.'

'No . . . no headache?'

'No. I never have headaches.'

'But . . . that . . . that pot fell on your head.'

'Yes, I know.' She held out a pile of crushed black straw. 'Look what it did to my hat.'

'Bugger your hat. Your brains should have been spewed over the floor. Why weren't they?'

'Don't be so awful. You make me feel sick.'

Martin crashed clenched fists down on to the arms of his chair and screamed.

'It's not bloody normal! When you fall off a lighthouse you're supposed to come to pieces. When a flaming great pot comes hurling down on yer bonce, you've no business to come prancing upstairs as though nothing had happened.'

She gave him a strange, inquiring look, then put what remained of her hat to one side.

'Didn't my mum tell you about me?'

'She only told me I'd put you in the pudding-club, and that turned out to be a lie.'

She laughed softly. 'That night you were drunk.'

'I certainly wouldn't have done it if I had been sober.'

She sighed and shook her head.

'Mum ought to have told you.'

'Told me what?'

'That I'm a Catomado.'

Martin held his breath for half a minute.

'Perhaps I shouldn't ask – what is a Catomado?'

Myna stared thoughtfully out of the window, then repeated her sigh.

'It's a secret – or supposed to be. But dad used to say: "Go to any town, walk down any street, knock on every door and the chances are one of them will be opened by a Catomado." '

Martin took a firm grip of his chair. 'But what the hell is a Catomado?'

Myna shrugged. 'A Catomado is – well – a Catomado. If one turns up in your family, you keep quiet about it. People aren't keen to know about us. I mean, to the ordinary person it's a bit off-putting to know we cannot be hurt if we fall ever so far, or if something ever so heavy falls on us. They get real narky when they realize we don't grow old, too.'

Martin made an awful growling sound. 'Never grow old?'

'No – we sort of curl up and fade away at the age of a hundred and four. It's known as tenty-fouring.'

'Tenty-fouring,' Martin repeated in an expressionless voice.

'Something very funny happened to me when I was a kid,' Myna went on. 'I got hit by an express train, and just bounced. But I have to eat lots of sausages; the seasoning's good for me.'

Martin tried to imagine a famine of sausages, a glorious dearth of bangers, but only succeeded in conjuring up a mental picture of a well-stocked butcher's shop. Then he became thoughtful. Why not?

There was a lot of careful planning and the outlay of quite a bit of money. Three knives – one large, one slender, one small. One saw and one chopper. Twenty-two yards of the best mutton-cloth, two scrubbing brushes, six bars of soap and three bottles of disinfectant. One large waterproof sheet. A pick-axe and spade. A large book of instructions. Most of his purchases he hid in the loft, but the book he kept to read in bed. Myna was curious. She read the title out loud.

' "Butchery for Beginners." Oh, are you going to make your own sausages?'

He thought for a moment.

'No,' he said at length. 'There'd be too many. I'd never find a buyer.'

'I'd try some,' Myna promised.

Martin had reason to doubt if that would be at all possible.

He caught her in the bath on Wednesday evening and had her nicely dismembered by eight o'clock next morning. He decided to spread the bits and pieces over a large area.

The left leg went into a rubbish tip near Clapham Junction; the right he donated to a hole under a tree in Bushy Park. Both arms went down a disused well near Sevenoaks. The torso was bulky and presented rather a problem, but eventually he slipped it into a sack, added some bricks, and dropped the end result over Hammersmith Bridge. The head was buried, on one dark night, in someone's front garden in East Sheen. Then he went home to worry.

The left leg came home on Friday morning.

Martin opened the front door, walked through into the kitchen, put his shopping bag down on the table – and there it was, upside down in the sink, trying to turn the cold tap on with its big toe. Martin said, 'Oh, dear!' then squealed like a mouse bidding farewell to a hungry cat, before fleeing to the bedroom, where he hurriedly locked the door. Time was to prove this was not an impregnable fortress.

The sun was setting when he heard the soft bumping sound on the fire-escape. Then the casement windows opened and the two arms undulated over the sill before flopping down on to the carpet. They began to wriggle towards him.

Once out of the bedroom, he made for the front door, but barely had he opened it when the right leg hopped in and made an unsuccessful attempt to stamp on his big toe. He took refuge in the lounge. As this was situated at the front of the building, there was no fire-escape, and Martin could only gaze down at a so-far-Myna-free street and ponder on the apparent adaptability of a Catomado.

Then a passing lorry slowed down and a moist, bulging sack oozed its way over the tailboard before falling to the road with an ominous clatter. It heaved, jumped, jerked, and finally rolled up over the kerbstone, across the pavement and down into a dark area. A crash of shattering glass. Myna's torso was in the basement – a little late, but then it had come a long way.

The lounge door shook under a series of soft bumps; the handle rattled, then turned, but the lock held firm. Martin wondered if the bits and pieces ever got tired. Did they need sleep or food? How could Myna eat sausages without a mouth? And that raised another point. Where was it?

The answer came in a most dramatic way. Something yo-yoed in front of the lounge window, then Myna's head settled on the sill. It flattened the already misshapen nose against the glass and grinned. Martin could do no less than throw a metal vase at it. He missed, of course, broke a window-pane, and the head seemed to nod its appreciation for this convenient means of entry. It leapt into the room and began to hop over the floor.

Legs are negative, arms lack personality, a torso has certain attributes, but a head which bounces is a force to be reckoned with.

Martin unlocked the door, tore into the hall, stumbled over a sack (which the arms were successfully untying), dodged a leg which tried to kick him, and hurled himself towards the front door.

He fell down one flight of stairs and ran down the rest, while ignoring a ridiculous urge to leap over the banisters. The tiled hall was waiting to receive him; the black and white squares were a chessboard over which he must move before the blessed safety of the street could be reached. His right foot landed on white, his left struck black – then he stumbled as a thought, a silly, nonsensical suggestion, made him look up. He was permitted one last, despairing shriek.

A round, hair-crowned ball was coming down. Its aim was perfect, and, as Martin was not a Catomado, his head split like an over-ripe melon.

Presently, Myna's head rolled over the tiled floor and began to bounce up the stairs.

The police inspector watched Martin's body being carried away, then turned and slowly mounted the stairs. When he reached the top landing he tapped on a door. It opened and Myna stood to one side so that he could enter. A jagged red line ringed her neck, and she was pale, but otherwise quite composed.

'He cut me up,' she said quietly.

For a full minute the inspector looked at her through narrowed eyes, then he asked:

'Are you a Catomado?'

She nodded. The inspector smiled.

'Same here.'

They gravely shook hands.

# DOROTHY DEAN

*Dorothy K. Haynes*

When Mrs Dean called at the Remand Home, shamefacedly and on foot, she was surprised to find it both respectable and anonymous. It was the kind of house where you might expect to find a brass plate, a doctor or dentist's or architect's; but only the brass bell glinted, and worn gilt on the fanlight scrawled the signature *Tintagel.*

The door was unlocked to admit her, and locked behind her again, and the Superintendent looked a cross between a hospital matron and a gaoler as she led the way to her room. Mrs Dean sat in the warm study, her white gloves screwed to grubbiness, her jersey suit smudged with train dust. Already, she was on the verge of breaking down. Only her indignation kept her going, a resentment against everyone concerned with placing Dolly in this halfway house between court and prison or, perhaps, if one dared to hope, a second chance in life.

'I can't understand it,' she said peevishly, forgetting that she had come to plead for help rather than to accuse. 'She's always been a good girl. She's highly strung; but what she did to Mrs Stanley, and then breaking up the room afterwards – well, I mean, it's just not *like* Dolly . . .'

'That's what we want to investigate,' said Miss Gallacher gently. 'We want to find out *why* she did it.' She felt that, at short notice, it was too much to expect her to unravel her charges' kinks for the benefit of persons who should have seen trouble coming a long time ago. The girls were here for such a short time. Some you were glad to see the last of, some you liked on sight; but you learned to distrust the lot of them: Veronica, with her bronzed hair turning to mouse; Barbara, who stole; Jean, who lost her head whenever a man looked at her, and Dolly Dean, who wouldn't talk, and who rejected all efforts to help her.

'We're having her checked up, of course,' she said. 'There's this nervous tic that she's got – '

'She can stop it if she wants to,' said her mother sharply. 'You don't need a doctor for that. It's not the first time I've smacked her out of a bad habit . . .'

She had always had some mannerism or other, like jerking her head or flicking her hair back. 'My hair gets in my eyes,' she complained, and so her mother clipped back her fringe and put the long mane into a pony-tail. Next there was blinking, screwing her eyes to squeeze the blackness till it ached ecstatically, but by this time she was at school, and they sent her to the eye clinic and made her wear glasses.

The blinking stopped, but it gave way to yet another habit, an uncomfortable twitch, to keep the glasses from sliding down her nose. She indulged in it when she was reading, and her mother would watch in exasperation, breaking in on her with complaints. 'You read far too much. Wasting your eyesight, that's what you're doing. No wonder you have to wear glasses.'

She sat reading all day in a dark corner, newspapers, comics or catalogues – whatever she could lay hands on. She spent long hours with Mrs Beeton; but her mother's library was limited. There was a more fascinating selection at Mrs Stanley's, and Mrs Stanley's house was itself an attraction. She lived across the landing, on the sunny side of the building, and her kitchen was bright with geraniums and green linoleum. Dolly went across sometimes to see the budgie. 'Wee Joey. Kiss wee Joey!' it chattered, and Mrs Stanley chattered back; and when they were both chattering away, Dolly would slip away from them and go into the parlour with the dark chenille curtains and the glass bookcase. There were old annuals there, *Chatterbox*, and musty, bound volumes of *Atalanta*, and the *Home Doctor*, banded with gold and too heavy to hold.

Dolly went through them all. The first time she opened the *Home Doctor* she was fascinated. There were men with stumps and moustaches, enduring terrible things; and then a folded diagram opened to show networks of nerves and arteries in a man stripped of skin . . .

She shut the book and locked the glass door, and for a long time she would not go back. Her mother could not understand it, nor could Mrs Stanley. 'I don't know,' she said. 'She just walked out without a word, as white as a sheet. Did she say anything to you?'

'No. Just that she didn't want to go back.'

But she went back, eventually, because she had to have another look; and when the first horror of the *Home Doctor* had spent itself, she discovered the book about martyrs, and this time she did not run from it, though it frightened her even more. The saints suffered willingly, too willingly, but they did not hide their pain. Wide mouths yelled, eyes rolled to Heaven. The pictures were red with fire and blood, but the saints did not die. They stayed screaming; and reading about it was worse than looking, because it told *everything*, the pincers and the burning, and how they dragged themselves about. She gnawed at her nails, trying to get the thought of it out of her mind.

'Don't bite your nails,' her mother said to her. '*And don't suck your thumb!* Honestly, Dolly, if it's not one thing with you, it's another!' She went to Mrs Stanley's to escape, and there, in the bookcase, was the scissor man, lean, leaping, and a child screaming in a shower of blood, or sprouting flames from every finger. *Struwwelpeter* said the sprawling letters, and she dreamed about it at night, but she did not tell her mother why she wakened and screamed. Her mother would have blamed it on her reading, and forbidden her to go to Mrs Stanley's again.

It was about this time that Mrs Stanley had what she liked to call, with a certain amount of pride, 'her accident'. A car battery that her husband, who was a garage attendant, had for some reason put on the top shelf of the cupboard, overturned and showered her with acid. She was alone at the time, but she managed to get to the door and shout for Mrs Dean. There was a great crying and running to and fro between the two houses, and for a while the doctor came every day; and then Mrs Stanley appeared again, as cheerful as ever, and looking almost the same. She had a tendency, however, to dwell on the accident, and Dolly saw her draw her blouse down and show the red weals on her breast before she covered them up tenderly again. She noticed the wry pull on her mouth as she touched the scars; and there was a blouse, a white blouse, eaten into holes, that was shown off sometimes to the gloating neighbours.

Dolly could not get the accident out of her head. Her mother and the other neighbours had taken turns at nursing her when she was in bed, and their whispers rolled down the echoing stairs: '. . . couldn't bear the blankets over her . . . marked for life. If you'd seen what I seen, Mrs . . . oh, I never knew a woman to suffer like that.'

Somehow, because of this, Dolly could not feel the same

towards Mrs Stanley. She was always afraid that she would draw her blouse down and show her scarred bosom; and yet she wanted to see . . .

She was always drawn to forbidden things. From the landing window, three stories high, she could see into the next back-yard, uneven with stones, and with great coarse dock plants sprouting in the corners. Her mother called it 'the dirty yard', and warned her not to go near it; but one day she stared and stared till she couldn't resist it any longer, and at last she climbed over the crumbling wall and into the forbidden land.

Her own window was high, high above; her own yard looked strange and unfamiliar. Here she could see into doors which from above were only shapes to her, wash-houses with dripping taps and broken tubs, and a dirty lobby stretching into darkness. A sour, soupy smell came from the lobby, and suddenly there was a man at her side, a thin, high-shouldered man in a dirty pink jersey.

She knew who he was. She had seen him from a distance, standing in the yard, with his high shoulders and tiny grey head. He was deaf and dumb, and nobody cared what happened to him. 'It's a shame,' her mother said. 'Three women next door, and not one of them sees that he gets a decent meal. He'd be better off in a home somewhere.'

For all that, she warned the child never to speak to him, never to speak to anyone from the dirty yard; and here he was now, his hand on her arm, grunting and making queer noises. His eyes were cold blue stones in a tiny skull. She screamed, and a fat woman in a rubber apron came and pulled him away. He shuffled over to a stone stair in the corner, and the woman shook her fist at him. Before Dolly could make up her mind to run, the woman had gone into her house and come back with a chunk of bread and rhubarb jam. 'Here, love,' she said coaxingly, and Dolly was afraid not to take it. She carried it back to her own yard, and there she dropped it in the dustbin.

She wanted to tell her mother about it, but she knew she would get into trouble for going, so she kept quiet, though she could not get the thought of the man out of her head. The house up the stone stairs had dirty windows, and she knew just what it would be like inside. She would lie in bed, seeing it: a furnace room with a black boiler taking up nearly all the space, and the floor all ashes. In the middle of the ashes the man would lie on an iron bed, blinking at the grey dark.

She did not know how she knew this. She did not like knowing. Then one day the bed was outside, poised on top of the stairs, and the man still in it. Rain fell on him, wind plucked at the covers, but he didn't move. With a sick horror on her, Dolly ran crying to her mother and told her to make the man go away. Her mother took one quick, astounded glance, and shook the child till she was stupid. 'There's no bed there, do you hear? There's nothing. Telling lies like that – you try that nonsense again, my girl, and I'll have something to say to you. The very idea!'

It was never mentioned again. Her mother did not believe in encouraging nonsense, and Dolly was afraid of her mother. She loved her, she ached with love of her, but somehow she could not talk to her. There was never time. Her mother had been rushed off her feet ever since she had been left a widow, and Dolly always came back from school to an empty house. The house was growing more and more neglected, dust on the dresser, spiders' webs in the corners, cold grease in the frying-pan. The mirrors were dim, and Mrs Dean never swept up the crumbs until Dolly was in bed; and Dolly was always glad to go.

Hunched up, eyes screwed, she would lie tense with a terrible pleasure, imagining things, the things she was afraid of: Mrs Stanley sizzling away in acid, the high-shouldered man doing horrible things, the saints with their eyes turned up and their mouths yelling. The pictures would come to her small, miles away, but so clear that they *rocked* with intensity; then they would rush together and explode in a black star, and she would feel herself trembling and somehow ashamed.

'Why don't you go out to play?' her mother said irritably. 'Mix with the other girls? Haven't you any friends at school?' She could not explain that at school the other girls laughed at her. Where authority saw her as a quiet child, sweet-faced and docile, her classmates saw only lank hair, glasses, and a tendency to fidget. Even the teachers could not ignore her fidgeting. 'For goodness' sake, Dolly, sit still. You'd think you had St Vitus' Dance.' Who was St Vitus? A long, deranged monk, continually on the twitch? Sometimes as she walked home alone he jerked and hobbled beside her, and when she got in she would sit quiet, so still that her mother noticed it; and dull as it was, she would wish that things could always be like that, because it pleased her mother.

She had a great and touching urge to be good. Sometimes she was happy, in a peculiar sort of way, as if she was living each day with an affecting devotion to everyone she loved. Surely, then, things had been happier, the times long ago, when she was small, and her mother took her on her knee and sang to her:

'Oh, Dorothy, Dorothy Dean,
Oh, Dorothy, where have you been?
She's suddenly flown
To regions unknown,
Along with a man on a flying machine.'

Funny how it came back to her, now, the old-fashioned song, through the racket of records the girls played in the Common Room, the heartsick crying of the Top Twenty and the pop charts. Funny how it frightened her, the Regions Unknown, sadder than anything wailed out by the boys with guitars . . .

'I just can't understand it,' said Mrs Dean querulously. 'She's had every chance. Of course, she's been left on her own a bit, but who hasn't? You've just got to trust them. You can't be around all the time.'

'Do you have to go out to work, Mrs Dean?'

'How else do you think we'd manage? It could be done, I suppose, but it would only be a bare living. I wanted to give her nice things, things I could never afford myself. And they *need* so much nowadays, record players, school trips – you just can't keep up with them . . . Not that Dolly ever asked for anything. She was quite happy, just reading and imagining things. I know some have said she'd too much imagination, but I saw to it that she kept it under control. I soon knocked the imagination out of her.'

'What did Dolly do when you were out, Mrs Dean?'

'Oh, she went over a lot to Mrs Stanley's. That's why I can't understand it. Ever since she could walk she's been in and out as if it was her own house. And Mrs Stanley wasn't the one to stand for a lot of nonsense either. There's no imagination about *her*. That's why I always felt she was so good for our Dolly . . .'

It was Mrs Stanley who first put the idea into her head. Dolly had gone over quite happily – but she did not look happy

She had a new mannerism now, a habit of peering round and rubbing her chin on her shoulder. There was no pleasure in it for her, nothing but an uncomfortable desire to do it once and for all and be finally rid of the temptation; but the temptation grew with every indulgence, until her mother sometimes slapped her in frustration, and the teachers checked her at school. It was time, everyone agreed, that Dolly grew out of that sort of thing, and Dolly knew it better than anyone.

This morning, Mrs Stanley took it on herself to do something about it. She started as soon as the girl came in, before she could lift a magazine from under the cushions.

'Do you know this, Dolly? People will think you've got something on your shoulder if you keep looking round like that. I knew a girl once that had a black imp on her shoulder. Nobody but her could see it, but she knew it was there, and she was always looking at it –'

'What happened to her?'

'The girl? Oh, I don't know. They took her away, I think. But she used to look round just like you –'

'I think I'll go back to my own house now,' said Dolly, her mouth tight, smiling, her heart nearly choking her.

She did not really believe there was an imp on her shoulder. She could not see it in the mirror. She stared in the smoky glass, and the room looked odd and fascinating, all the furniture back to front, and her face not at all as she imagined it. Her cheeks were red, guiltily red, her hair dark, and her tongue sly-pointed at the edge. Suppose the imp *was* there? She jerked her head sideways, to surprise it, and thought she saw the flick of a black tail; but it was only her hair, flung round. There was nothing. Of course there wasn't. Then, sitting quiet at the fireside, reading her book, she felt it on her shoulder, the slight weight and warmth of it, and a sweat came out on her as she sat rigid, waiting for it to move.

'Will you set the plates for me, Dolly?'

'Mummy . . .' She said it experimentally, her voice casual, but with screaming undertones. 'Mummy, there's something on my –'

'What, dear?' Her mother was at the sink, peeling the potatoes, her mind already on the next task, and Dolly knew that she would never be able to tell.

'Nothing,' she said, and went carefully, steadily, to the table.

In time, her mother noticed it. 'What are you holding your

shoulder like that for?' she asked, irritable at always having to criticize. 'Your left shoulder's higher than your right. Have you got a stiff neck, or what?'

'No. No – it's all right.' Dolly relaxed carefully, so as not to disturb the resting fiend.

'If it's not one thing, it's another. Why you've got to get up to all these capers, I don't know . . .'

She walked at a slow, gliding pace, because she was afraid that a jerk might send the invisible thing flying. Or would it only dig in its claws? She was afraid to put it to the test. It was like having an animal that could be vicious, but what kind of an animal she didn't know. Black, maybe, with sharp ears and a bat's wings and a tail like a devil's?

Her mother poked the fire, and flirted the brush from the companion set.

'Do you *feel* anything wrong with your shoulder?'

'It – it feels heavy. As if there was something on it.'

'Well, there isn't. And the quicker you get those ideas out of your head, the better.'

But her mother was wrong. The weight shifted, the clutch of small feet tightened, and sometimes there was a warmth of breath at her ear. Once or twice she put up a hand to feel, but there was nothing – unless it had edged away. It seemed able to move. At night, reluctantly, it let her undress, but in bed it sat, touching her, on the pillow. And all the time she wanted to tell about it.

There was sun in Mrs Stanley's kitchen, and she blamed her mother because their house was at the dark side of the building

'Oh, come in, Dolly. My, what's wrong with your shoulder?'

It's nothing . . .' She walked in, casual and cautious, but her voice went high with the effort of not tilting the fiend. 'Any magazines, Mrs Stanley?'

'There might be one or two. Go and have a look.' She handed her a biscuit from the tin, pink mallow and coconut. 'You're a great girl for the books. How are you getting on at school?'

'Fine, thank you.' She chewed the biscuit, but the crumbs went dry in her mouth. 'Mrs Stanley, remember that girl with the black imp?'

'What girl, dearie?'

'The girl that used to look round like me.' Her voice broke and she swallowed. 'And you said she'd an imp on her shoulder.'

'Oh, that one? I don't know. Nobody knew for sure that there *was* an imp. It was just the way she kept looking round, and people said – '

'Mrs Stanley, I think there's one on my shoulder!' It was out now, in tears and wild panic. 'I know I kept looking round, but it wasn't for that, honest it wasn't! I just did it because . . . I just did it! But now I feel one there . . .'

Mrs Stanley smoothed her skirt, and swallowed two or three times. Her eyes, fearful suddenly, looked over the child. 'Tell me where it is,' she said nervously. '*I* can't see anything.'

'No, but neither could the other girl. And neither can I. But I can *nearly* see it. Just here . . .'

'Oh, get away with you!' Mrs Stanley was becoming more confident. 'You've far too much imagination. I – I was just kidding about that other girl. I said it to get you to stop that habit you've got.'

'I can't stop. I can't stop now it's there.'

'But it isn't there! Did you tell your mother about it?'

'No. She'd have been angry. She shook me when I told her about the man in the bed – '

'What man?' said Mrs Stanley sharply, almost eagerly.

'The man in the dirty yard. He used to lie in bed, on the stairs. I could see him . . . there was a furnace in his room, and he used to get burnt squeezing past – ' She could not stop herself, the horrors mounting, crowding out of her mouth to the woman who did not want to hear . . .

Mrs Stanley went white, and the sunlight in the room seemed to sicken. Jerkily, she went over to the window and craned out. There was the shabby yard, the stone stairs and the iron railing; but there was not a bed to be seen, and no room for one on the landing – and the deaf man had been taken to a home long ago.

'You're making it up,' she said. 'You imagined it.'

'I know,' said the child. 'But it comes into my mind and frightens me, and it's *there*. And now there's this imp – you shouldn't have *told* me – '

'I know what'll happen to you.' Mrs Stanley picked up her duster nervously, and inched her way among the ornaments. 'There's a place for people who let their imaginations run away with them. I remember one girl who was always making up stories. She got so she didn't know what was real and what wasn't, and one day they came for her in a black van – '

'No!' Dolly screamed, seeing the van draw up, knowing that if Mrs Stanley said so, it would be so. There was desolation and terror in knowing that now, at last, she had gone too far. She lifted a knife, a poker, a candlestick, she didn't know what it was, and screamed and screamed as she went for her; and somehow there was a queer pleasure in it, the twisted pleasure of the martyr book and the cruelty of *Struwwelpeter*.

Nobody scolded. Everyone was very kind as they took her, Dolly, back to her own house, and her mother, and the people who came for her in a closed van. And now all she felt was the desire to be safe and good. She was played out and weary, and chastened at the thought of what she had done. But it would be all right. She could behave if she wanted to. She sat quiet and conscious of her self-restraint, and there was nothing on her shoulder. She looked round, she moved her shoulder, but the imp had gone. Surely that was a good sign? Surely, if she did what they told her, they would let her go home . . . She thought of her mother, her face tired, her hands tired, and her mouth squared with the strain of not crying. All she had to do was to run into her arms, and never let go as her mother petted her:

'Oh, Dorothy, Dorothy Dean,
Oh, Dorothy, where have you been . . . ?'

Her mother was standing with Miss Gallacher, all dressed up for visiting, with her pearls on, and her navy suit, and her gloves all grubby with train dust, and as soon as Dolly saw her she knew that she was angry. 'Well? I hope you've been behaving yourself. You'll have to pull yourself together, you know, if they let you out of here . . .'

It went on like that all the time. She did not cry when the visit was over, and her mother gone, still indignant and hurt. Stiff, icy cold, she sat alone, and there was nothing behind her, nothing good or bad to remember, and nothing to look forward to or dread. And then, suddenly, there was a slight pressure on her shoulder, a warmth of hair or fur on her face. For a second, she almost saw it; and then it settled down, invisible but familiar. The fiend, the friend, its weight no longer a burden, and its touch a caress.

# HOTHOUSE

*Sydney J. Bounds*

For eleven miles after leaving Bredan village, the tarmac road wound between hedgerows that screened distant cows and lonely trees. Farther on, Howard Parker glimpsed a pair of open wrought-iron gates and slowed his car. Approaching them, he read a name-plate: *The Plantation*, and swung between the gates, following the drive up to the house. He switched off the motor and climbed stiffly from behind the wheel.

The house was big and old, in need of repair. Parker climbed stone steps and hammered twice with a rusty iron knocker, then waited, looking about him. The grounds were wooded, extensive, and in need of care. It was so quiet that he became aware of his own breathing; and, self-conscious, he adjusted his knitted-wool tie and buttoned the cord jacket.

A tall, lugubrious-faced man wearing an apron came round a corner of the house from the direction of the gardens. 'Yes, sir? Can I help you?'

Parker offered a pasteboard card which the man scrutinized. '"Organic Fertilisers . . ." The Colonel told me to expect you. This way, sir.'

Parker followed the man round the outside of the house, along a flagstoned veranda with cobwebs between the pillars, towards a large domed building. Weak sunlight glinted off hundreds of glass panes; the interior lay hidden behind a dense panoply of broad green leaves. The woodwork had been newly painted.

Heat leaked out as the door opened. Beyond was a kind of air-lock and another door. When this opened, heat struck like the blast from a furnace.

Parker's mouth gaped involuntarily to suck in a lungful of damp, scent-laden air. He stepped into a green gloom of steamed-over windows, moved between giant sprays of fern and hanging vines and bamboo stems. Exotic flowers blazed magenta and yellow-on-white and violet-blue, hiding an array of metal pipes.

In a central clearing was a wicker chair in which an old man reclined; with faded hair and limp moustache he appeared

Dresden-fragile, dehydrated. Palm leaves sheltered and almost obscured him. The sharply-pointed spines of woody canes threatened his translucent flesh like a battery of hypodermic needles.

'This is Mr Parker, Colonel. Representing Organic Fertilisers.'

Colonel West stared with intense, brooding eyes, gestured with a bony finger. 'Sit down, Mr Parker. A drink for our guest, Johns. You will take port, sir?'

Parker collapsed into a wicker seat, mopping sweat, his clothes sticking to him. 'A long one, please – plenty of lemonade.'

The door opened with a swirl of humid air, closed again.

'You are looking at my life's work,' Colonel West said. 'I've hunted plants all over the tropics, learnt a few things, too. Now I've retired, it pleases me to sit among the things I enjoy. There's more to plants than you might think, Mr Parker.'

Johns returned bearing a tall glass on a silver tray. Parker, wilting, took it and sipped gratefully.

'Borneo,' the Colonel continued reminiscently. 'I remember the Monkeycups there – a pitcher plant. The pitcher leaves fill with rain water in which insects drown. The plant absorbs the insects. Ingenious really.

'You can have no grasp of the prolificity of plants unless you've been in a rain forest. A path will be grown over as fast as you clear it. Stand still for only a few minutes and you can see them grow. Plenty of sun, plenty of rain . . . and, of course, natural fertilisers. Organic. Plants need that. Animals drop where they die, the ground absorbs their juices, plants grow.'

Colonel West relaxed, the intenseness faded from his eyes.

'It is discourteous to keep you here so long, Mr Parker. Excuse an old man's rambling. I need manure and I've no faith in chemicals. You can supply a range of organic fertilisers?'

Parker loosened his tie desperately, gasping, 'Made up to your requirements.'

'I want blood – can't beat blood for healthy plants. How do you sell it?'

'By the hundredweight. Balanced compounds, unless otherwise specified.'

'What kind of blood?'

'Bullocks, calves, sheep or pigs.'

'I'll take five hundredweight initially. Compound. Bullocks' blood, thirty per cent.'

Parker drained his glass, scribbled a notation with sweaty fingers. 'Thirty per cent blood . . . thank you, sir.' He rose, dodging vines. 'I'll arrange delivery for next week.'

He jerked open the door and stumbled into fresh air, gasping with relief.

Three months passed before Parker called again at *The Plantation*, in answer to a fresh inquiry from the Colonel. The grounds appeared even more neglected, the house even more run down. As he used the iron knocker, flakes of rust fell away.

Worry deepened the lines on Johns's lugubrious face.

'I'm glad to see you, sir. The Colonel doesn't leave the hothouse at all these days – you're the first visitor in over a month. Perhaps –' Johns hesitated. 'You'll notice a difference. I'm afraid he's not long to go.'

They moved along the flagstoned path, weeds growing between cracks. The domed greenhouse sparkled in sunlight, a cherished island in a sea of neglect.

Although Parker anticipated the heat as the inner door opened, it still hit him. He stepped into the aquarium-gloom, confronting a barrage of giant fronds studded with blood-red and yellow and violet. He couldn't see the Colonel at first, so buried was he under foliage, shrouded by a curtain of vines. The cloying scent of blooms in that damp heat made Parker gag.

He fumbled his way to a seat opposite the Colonel, a frail figure with waxen skin.

'My plants are doing well, young man. A good mixture your people made up. I'm pleased with it – pleased with you.'

Johns returned with port and lemon and Parker drank thirstily. He watched fascinated as spiked stems drooped and hovered above the Colonel, settled on his bare skin like insects coming to rest.

Colonel West seemed not to notice. 'The orchids are doing especially well. Heat. Water. Fertiliser. The reason I asked you to call – I want another five hundredweight delivered as soon as you can. Stick to bullocks' blood, but double the amount this time. Sixty per cent blood. You can do that?'

'Of course, sir.' Parker made a note. 'I suggest not too near the stems.'

The brooding eyes flashed. 'Don't tell me how to feed plants!' He sank back, exhausted.

Parker said, mildly alarmed, 'I'm sorry, sir. Of course you

know best . . . Perhaps I'm tiring you?'

The Colonel barked a laugh. 'Johns been worrying you, has he? He's a bit of an old maid. Take no notice – I don't intend to die!'

Parker gulped the rest of his drink. 'Delivery in three to four days, sir – and thank you.'

He hurried to escape, feeling uncomfortable in a way that had nothing to do with the temperature.

Parker forgot about Colonel West until the laboratory asked him to look in to check the result of the new mixture. Passing close to Bredan he decided, reluctantly, that he'd best get it over with. He followed the tarmac road to *The Plantation*, drove between the still-open gates and stopped in front of the house.

A gloomy silence hung over the grounds. He climbed the steps and used the knocker; no one came. Finally he tried the door and it swung open at his touch.

'Mr Johns?'

His voice echoed emptily in the hall. Unmarked dust lay on the floor. The air smelt musty, as though the house had been deserted for some time.

Parker waited, uncertain, then walked round the side of the house towards the greenhouse. He saw immediately some broken panes, a tangle of creepers thrusting out. A solid wall of green leaves prevented him from seeing inside.

The outer door opened easily; the heat was no more than a gentle warmth. He had to exert force on the inner door and, when it gave, the stink hit him. He peered through a jungle of leaves and creepers, bamboo stems and exotic blossoms.

'Colonel? Colonel West?'

It seemed idiotic to call out. No one could be in there now. Johns would never have left without a powerful motive.

But some inner unease prompted Parker to push forward, force a passage through the wild and tangled growth. He brushed aside ferns and palm leaves and advanced towards the centre of the forest of plants.

He saw the wicker chair and, in it, a figure reclining motionless, smothered beneath a network of lianas.

'Colonel West!'

The still figure made no reply. Parker pushed closer, frowning. The body of the Colonel was bloated, the flesh tinged with green. Long, sharp spines pierced his skin, reaching to the veins. Parker detected a faint pulse.

The eyes moved, watching him. The lips parted in a smug smile.

## THE OLD MEN

*Julia Birley*

'So then I said, whatever did she take me for? I mean, a girl who'd accept a double blind date in this hospital would accept anything, wouldn't she? Sorry, dear, we didn't realize you were in the bed – move over now, and we'll make you all comfy . . .'

It was an ordinary, peaceful morning on the Women's Surgical Ward. It might even have been silent but for the chatter of the two nurses, whisking from bed to bed. The young house surgeon could hear every word from inside the drawn curtains where he was engaged, under Sister's critical eye, in removing someone's stitches. The talk went past the cubicle and crossed to the opposite side. 'Funny!' they were saying. 'However many beds you make, there always seems to be one more. I could have sworn we'd done this one.' 'And look at the state it's in. Must be Mrs Grimes, the old so-and-so.' 'No, Mrs Grimes is number seven. But look here, Katy, this one was empty when we went off duty.' 'Well, in that case, all I can say is, we must have had an octopus admitted in the night!'

At the sound of their giggles, Peter Wells glanced up and caught the beady eye of Sister Hopkin. He blushed for no particular reason, and wondered why they went unreproved. All this was no concern of his, and yet –

He laid the bedclothes back in place and followed Sister out of the cubicle. Both knew that there had been no new admission in the night; neither made any comment. But Peter caught sight of the bed in question just before it was stripped. Empty as it was, there was something most unpleasant about it, the sheets creased this way and that, the pillows not merely dented but grubby, as pillows in a good hospital are never seen to be. He could understand the glances the nurses exchanged, the rigidity of their neat figures.

He left in a hurry, as usual. It was just one of the small, inexplicable events that had been bugging him somehow, getting on his nerves ever since he came to St Cyprian's. The sheer size of the place was part of the trouble, he thought, as he tramped the enormous length of corridor connecting old buildings still in use with the imposing new surgical block, the clinics and lecture rooms. The general design was more of a web than a honeycomb, centred on the great rotunda full of echoing footsteps; the surrounding passages consequently took the form of a curve. As he strode from theatre to canteen to ward and back again, the hordes of people walking in front or behind were invisible, because of the curve, at only a few yards' distance. This, Peter found, induced claustrophobia, and tended to give him funny ideas, such as that of being followed along those windowless, all-concealing corridors by a particular pair of feet, whose heavy, mechanical tread might or might not be some kind of echo. 'He' (if the feet really had an owner) was very noticeable late at night, after Peter's last round, when the two of them would be walking alone under the quiet lights. Peter would go briskly on, hoping he would get adequate sleep that night, knowing there was no time to waste on fancies. For once, in the daytime, he had heard those plonking feet more distinctly than usual among a lot of others coming away like himself from a late lunch. He leant on a radiator and waited. A bevy of orderlies clattered past; the one he was listening for must have stopped just around the curve, near the Orthopædic Centre. He could even see a shadow. He went swiftly round – and a pale girl, parked in a wheelchair, looked up, startled, as he pounced towards her.

It had been very well at first to pretend to himself that he noticed nothing, that there was nothing to notice. The work was exacting. He was universal dogsbody on a firm where the boss, as he had soon found out, was an unpredictable tyrant. Everyone's nerves were permanently on edge, so why not his? Was he even really alone in feeling that some kind of trickster was loose among them? The look in Sister Hopkin's eye, and the nurse's remark, 'There always seems to be one more,' came back with the memory of a grimy, rumpled bed that no one had slept in. In the corridors, the lecture room, the wards, it was just the same. Above all, in the operating theatre, as the group round the table grew and diminished, nurses and porters stepping in and out of the circle of light; again and again, instead of keeping his eyes fixed on the drama in the centre, he would find himself glancing covertly at all those other eyes above the various masks. Some, as always, he could identify; others were unknown. He could never tell which was the intruder, the one who had no business inside the theatre: only that an intruder of some kind was there. Well, so what? Even if his hunch was correct, what did it matter?

The day came when he had to ask that question rather more urgently. He was scrubbing up before an operating session, along with the two registrars, and demanding their sympathy rather loudly for a complaint that his free weekend had been cancelled. The younger of them, a reticent girl called Hazel Button, nudged him warningly. All three heard unmistakable sounds of someone moving in the instrument room, and a clang from the sterilizer.

Mr Eckstein, the senior registrar, went forward to investigate. They had seen no one go in, and, as it turned out, no one was there now. But as he approached the sterilizer, the other two saw him stumble in an ungainly fashion most unlike his usual precise movements. His right arm pushed away the lid, which had been loosened, and plunged into the boiling water.

Miss Button and Peter ran to his aid as he reeled back, yelling with pain. In the confusion, Peter thought he heard the victim say, 'So now it starts on me!' But professional control soon reasserted itself; he fell silent, nursing his hand, while Miss Button went off to begin the morning's list. Peter helped him downstairs to the Casualty Department, and when it was clear that the hand was badly scalded and would not be usable for many days, Eckstein permitted himself one dour comment: 'Monty will have to stir his stumps.'

This remark at least his junior understood. Monty, alias Montagu Cope, FRCS, consultant surgeon, was one of the 'old men' of St Cyprian's, who held the keys to promotion and success. To young Peter, they appeared as a wordly and powerful clique, capable of sitting to eternity in the godlike positions they had won, protecting each other from the competition of crude young talent. Intrigues and enmities they might have among themselves – for instance, there was Dr Hunter-Bevis, with his silver side-burns and gold cuff-links, who had built up a valuable private practice in days when good connections went farther than clinical merit. The bearded and colourful Monty despised him quite openly, and could never refrain from sarcastic comments on his case-histories. But let any outsider threaten, and these two rogues smiled on one another like brothers. They had all the affable solidarity of a Mafia, and, enjoying the good things life had been pleased to grant them, they imposed all they possibly could on their juniors. These, rushed off their feet, and in no position to rebel, all tended to obey one simple commandment: 'Thou shalt not stick thy neck out except in desperation.' Nothing therefore was said, even among themselves, about Eckstein's very peculiar mishap. As for those whispers about a poltergeist, or something of the sort, which seemed to be going the rounds from ward to kitchen, office or sluice – well, doctors are rationalists. Peter perceived that it was expedient for him, as for the others, to pretend it was all beneath his notice.

On the next operating morning, he went to summon Mr Cope from his room, to perform a delicate anastomosis that was beyond Miss Button's skill. He was surprised, as he reached the door, to hear a great rattling from inside, as though it had been locked, but when he touched the handle, it opened at once. There emerged then, not Mr Cope but Dr Hunter-Bevis himself. Peter politely inquired if he was all right, and was answered, 'No, dammit!' in such quavering tones that he felt obliged to keep pace with the old man as he shuffled down the corridor. 'This is the pay-off!' he was muttering. Clearly something worse than a jammed door must have put him out.

A moment later, he rounded on Peter as if he must talk to someone. 'I know you, don't I? You're on Monty's firm? Well your chief back there has seen my X-rays, and he wants to carve me up. What do you think of that, eh?'

So that was it. There had been a professional consultation; besides, the yellow face of old HB showed that all was not well inside him. Peter laughed diplomatically, and asked what he could say, even if he had seen the X-rays, which privilege had not been his. Then he looked serious, and praised Mr Cope's skill. 'Oh, I know, I know,' groaned the physician. 'Save it for the patients, Wells. You know I can't insult him by taking my custom elsewhere.'

Peter saw his point and, back in the theatre, concealed an unkind grin behind his mask. Mafia law forbade that anyone but a colleague should undertake the fairly straightforward operation he surmised HB might need. But to have to submit to Monty's scalpel, after being so long and so often dissected, as it were, by his scornful tongue! One could almost feel sorry for the old quack.

Cope was slow in arriving and long in making his preparations. He liked to give himself the prima donna airs of a bygone generation: of the 'wizard with the knife'. He made his entrance at last in impressive silence, swathed from head to foot, holding out his shapely hands with a hieratic gesture for the dresser to put on the gloves. Over the mask, his cold blue eyes surveyed his retinue, headed by Peter and the Theatre Sister, waiting respectfully each side of the prepared victim. (Only Dr Banner, the anæsthetist, another of the 'old men', sat coolly reading the paper and holding a limp wrist.) The surgeon would point to the instrument he needed and, if it was satisfactory, would make little passes over the exposed abdomen, like an artist coquetting with his brush. Then, as he fell to work, he would begin a running commentary, joking in his harsh way if his mood were good, or, if not, reducing many a nurse to tears and Peter to a sweating sycophancy he was afterwards ashamed to recall.

For who was Monty Cope, after all? A rich old bachelor, it was said, living it up in St John's Wood or Hampstead, competent at his job, but Eckstein was cleverer, and certainly much easier to work with. Today, when Monty ought to have been tickled pink at the thought of carving up HB within the next few weeks, he seemed to be in a fury. He threw four scalpels on the floor in quick succession, and when a junior nurse gave a hysterical titter, ordered her in foul terms to leave the theatre. 'I am not required to operate in the presence of fools,' he hissed. 'Of which we have one too many in here today. Go on, get out. I mean you.'

The session became an exhausting penance. When all was over, gowns peeled off, brows mopped, and Monty's hair and beard, if not his temper, smooth once more, he detained his junior registrar and houseman with a commanding grunt and led them back to his consulting room. 'Perhaps one of you would care to explain *this*!' He pointed to the newly-painted wall above his desk, and they saw, with amazement, what had annoyed him in the first place. The wall was covered with straggling handwriting, in great uneven letters.

*'hallo monty* (it read) *here i am you see a little stronger each day I told you it would take time your new boy is in a flat spin and many more in this hospital now hb is a sick man so expect the payoff i say cope you took my job and my guts but i will have your job and somebody elses guts so look out for you know who'*

Peter could barely decipher the scrawl, which struck him as meaningless drivel. Cope apparently thought otherwise. 'I did not notice it, strangely enough, when I entered the room this morning, but Dr Hunter-Bevis, of course, drew my attention to it as soon as he came in. Pray, which of you two is responsible?'

Miss Button indignantly denied the charge for both. At first he was too enraged to listen. 'Don't give me that! Only one other person in the world could have done it – three months ago. As you are well aware, he is not in a position to do it this morning.'

She bowed her head and stood looking at her neat shoes.

'It will be painted out,' he continued, less sure of his ground. 'But that does not atone for the insult to myself and my colleague. He is, as it happens, suffering from gall-stones. I shall perform a cholecystectomy after Christmas. To add to his natural – er, agitation, the joker had contrived to lock us both in. It was you, Wells, who opened the door.'

'None the less,' Miss Button insisted, 'this had nothing to do with either of us.'

For a moment the grizzled beard continued to point at them accusingly. Then, perhaps realizing the futility of his suspicions, Cope smiled disarmingly. 'Well, it hardly seemed likely – no desire to cut your own throats, eh? But I had to ask. May I, by way of reparation, invite you to a little party at my place on New Year's Eve?'

In the passage outside, Peter seized the girl's arm. 'You were marvellous, Hazel. But what on earth does it all mean?'

'I shall be surprised if we ever know.'

'Did HB do it? Or even Monty himself? And who is this other person who could have done it three months ago? Sometimes I think everyone here is round the bend.'

She regarded him gravely. 'You're not the only one. I've done nothing but apply for jobs elsewhere since I came. But we can't talk here. Let's go to the pub round the corner.'

Peter enjoyed his beer and sandwich more than usual. He

had never really heard Hazel talk before; up till now, her remarks had been of the order of 'sutures, please,' and 'now we expose the Pouch of Douglas.' Today she was almost voluble. She had not the least idea, she said, who the joker could be who seemed to be upsetting the hospital in all kinds of ways. But plenty of people had plenty of grievances, while other people were certainly afraid of what might come out if there were investigations. Peter could very well be right in one of his guesses. These two old men both had consciences that might explain some sort of hysterical outburst, she would have thought.

Peter was not satisfied, but he did not argue. They were both anxious for an explanation that fitted normal experience. He went on to ask why Cope had suspected, or pretended to suspect, themselves?

'Oh – you, because you opened the door, and because he is always suspicious of promising young men. Me, because I was there when Dr Litchfield died. Who was Dr Litchfield? Well, there are reasons why you might not have heard of him. He was chief pathologist here, a clever, violent sort of man, with red hair. He and Monty used to be very thick; they had all sorts of orgies and intrigues together.' She grimaced. 'But they fell out over an inquest on a case where HB had boobed more egregiously than usual. He'd refused to sign a death certificate for a patient who turned out to have a pericardial effusion, which any houseman could have spotted in his sleep. Litchfield did the p.m., and showed up HB's incompetence as publicly as possible. All the "old men" were after his blood then, but it was Monty who got him the sack. Focused attention on how he'd fiddled his department's accounts from the day he was appointed. He had no choice but to resign. Perhaps Monty had been looking for a chance to shed him – anyway, they all closed ranks, and he was shed. On boards and places where they meet, their unanimity is wonderful.'

'You sound very bitter.'

'I have good cause. Monty's made it quite plain that I don't get a reference until I share his bed, the old goat. Don't look so shocked. It's time you knew how these things were managed.'

Somewhat perturbed, Peter asked, 'What happened to Litchfield?'

'Well, he must have felt he'd had it. He was getting on in

years, a bit of an alcoholic. His prospects were bleak. He went to the pharmacy and poured just about every poison he could find down his throat – except strychnine, or anything that would have done the job efficiently. And then he came all the way back to the rotunda, walking like a robot. I heard him even before I saw him. I was coming through from E Block, and I heard this tramping – ' Peter nodded; he knew what it was like. 'And he came and stood in front of Reception. His face was shiny white, like a toadstool, his eyes sort of bulging. We thought he must be having some kind of fit. But he waved us back, and then he caught sight of me and said, quite distinctly, "Miss Button, tell Monty I've gone through the whole process. They won't escape now. Monty knows – " Then suddenly he doubled over, and – ' She paused a moment, then continued calmly, 'Well, he fell down, and I can best describe it unprofessionally by saying that he burst. You see, the lining of the stomach – '

Peter nodded again, with a show of medical interest. He did not finish his beer. He agreed to say nothing to anyone about the writing on Cope's wall.

Christmas came and went quite peacefully. Perhaps the goodwill released on all sides would have been powerful enough to drive out the poltergeist altogether – if only it could have lasted. But it was gradually drowned in floods of intemperance, followed by hangovers, and then, on New Year's Eve, a wan Peter was obliged to make his way to Mr Cope's smart house. He was not looking forward to the party, though he was curious to see the man off duty.

The ornate front door was opened by Cope himself, wearing a spangled shirt and clearly in a festive mood. Loud music followed him from a room almost totally dark, where there seemed to be dancing. He was not visibly enthusiastic at the sight of Peter, and might have forgotten inviting him.

'I was just going to ring the hospital and ask you to look in on one or two cases for me. But as you seem to be off duty, you may as well stay and have a drink. You can go back in an hour or so.' Then he shot out an arm and caught hold of a woman who had just come out of the dark room, and bent down, tickling her bare midriff with his beard. 'What a delicious spleen!' he crooned. 'Don't let anyone but me take it out for you, hm?'

This, Peter found, set the tone of the evening, which

appeared to have been arranged chiefly as an ego trip for the host. His women, with bodies as seductive as their eyes were calculating, made the young man feel callow and inhibited. It was a relief to catch sight of Hazel, cornered by some paunchy type and obviously in need of rescue. They danced together in the dark, and he was beginning to feel quite a dog after all, when he suddenly remembered Monty's orders and found to his disappointment that it was nearly twelve.

'Shall I just forget?' he suggested, but Hazel thought, better not. She wanted to go back with him anyway.

They found Monty in his study, which had been arranged as a bar. 'Bless you, my children!' he cried with false heartiness. 'Going already? But I'm glad you looked in. I wanted to show you a little souvenir that should interest you as it does me.'

He twinkled, and his beard wagged roguishly as he lifted a sealed jar from the corner cupboard and placed it before them. 'What do you make of those?' he asked Peter.

'Morbid intestines.'

'Ye-es. Whose?'

Peter had no idea. Hazel was afraid she knew, but was too wary to say so.

'See the discoloration? That's a unique phenomenon. There's an unidentified toxin in those intestines, among several others that are quite familiar. Now, Litchfield wrote a suicide note to Hunter-Bevis and myself, which unfortunately I can't show you because it remains in the hands of the Law. In this note, he claimed to have taken a drug whose effect, in combination with known poisons, would be to enable the soul to leave the body intact at the moment of death! Ha, that's news to you, Miss Button, isn't it? Well, of course, they looked hard for whatever it was, but they never found it. He must have drunk all he made.'

He discoursed learnedly on the probable physical action of the drug, and the reasons why the local pathologists had failed to analyze it. 'When they gave up, I asked leave to take it to one of the big firms, but they weren't very interested. So it has returned to me for the present. I'm not sure what I shall do with it.'

But as he bent to peer at the jar, there was an expression of triumph on his saturnine face. They guessed that he would never allow this curio out of his possession. It gave him too much pleasure to have it.

Peter said not a word as they left the house and drove back to St Cyprian's in Hazel's car. As they drew up, he announced his conclusion: 'There really is something evil about those old men.'

'You're very young, Peter,' she was beginning, but he answered, 'Not so much of that!' and took her in his arms.

On entering the rotunda, however, their happy mood evaporated. They looked at each other, knowing that with the New Year the unpleasant, threatening atmosphere was back again. 'Oh dear,' sighed Hazel. 'I ought to go and get those samples from the path. lab., and I really don't fancy it after all we've been hearing. Would you come with me?'

'I'll go instead,' he told her, and set off at once, to get it over.

The passage to Dr Litchfield's old laboratory was the narrowest, longest and grimmest in the whole of St Cyprian's. It was nicknamed Stiffs' Alley by the callous, because it led right underneath the new buildings, across the street and into the old block by way of the mortuary. There was always a possibility of having to flatten yourself against the wall while a solemn porter wheeled a covered trolley past, sad evidence of the limits of medical skill.

Normally, Peter had no special feelings about this passage, but tonight he certainly did not like the way it echoed his footsteps, almost from the moment he entered it, with a familiar mechanical tramping far behind. But here at least there was no curve. He had only to turn his head to see what was coming – if indeed something was! But it was an effort to do this. He achieved it only because the thing seemed to be catching up with him.

Thank heaven, only a porter with a trolley! But hadn't he rather forgotten the dignity of the occasion? He bore down on Peter in such an uncommon hurry to get past that there was barely time to squeeze out of the way. Nor could the onlooker fail to notice the strange shape under the sheet, which appeared to be moving. He raised his eyes to the man's sweating face. 'What have you got there, Sims?'

'God's truth, I'm glad to see you, Doctor. It's not fair on a man. I get a call to Ward Six, to fetch a body quickly. I go up, but Sister's nowhere about, just the trolley left in the side ward. It was right enough when I started, that I'll swear.

Perhaps you'd take a look, sir? No doubt one of you young gentlemen's having a prank with me.'

This put Peter on his mettle, and, despite a strong repugnance, he attempted to fold back the sheet. Immediately an enormous ginger car jumped out from beneath and fled in front of them down the tunnel. Of the reputed corpse there was so sign.

'Ah!' breathed the porter. 'That's the finish, that is. Twenty years I've been here, but I'm getting my cards tomorrow.'

'What, for a New Year's joke?'

But Sims stared him down. 'I said that for the record. I didn't expect either of us to believe it. There was a body when I started all right. Drunk on duty, you'd call me. You have to take the handiest explanation, or where would you all be? I'm getting out before the worst happens.'

This was the most direct statement Peter had heard, and he would have liked to discuss the whole thing with Hazel. But when they were alone together he wanted to make love to her, not waste time arguing. For she would certainly reach for the handiest explanation.

The next evening they had a date, which turned out quite unprofessional and finished up at her place in the small hours, when she said she must throw him out as they were both due to attend the removal of a piece of HB that very morning.

'Hazel, darling, let's have another orgy very soon.'

'Of course.' She added thoughtfully, 'Why should the devil have all the good tunes?'

She looked as spruce as ever, scrubbing up a few hours later, but Peter was somewhat dazed with lack of sleep, and though Mr Cope was operating and he would have little to do, he felt it would be a great relief when the morning was over. He was on his way out to fetch his chief from the consulting-room when he was delayed by the arrival of the patient himself, who was wheeled in, still awake, and reaching out his hand for the young man to grasp.

'Ah, Wells, is that you?' Hunter-Bevis mumbled anxiously. 'I dreamt about you last night. You were wheeling me along Stiffs' Alley – do they still call it that? We used to, Monty and I –'

'He'll be here quite soon, Dr Hunter-Bevis. Now here is Dr Banner to give you your injection.'

'Yes, I know, I know. But wait a minute, I want to ask you something.' And he dragged at Peter's white coat until he bent down, then whispered, 'I suppose it was you who put that writing on Monty's wall, saying you'd take his job? Well, I want you to know I'm quite willing. Do the operation yourself, now, before he gets here. I'd feel safer – ooh!'

At that moment, Dr Banner, losing patience, had given him the injection. He sank to sleep, still clutching Peter's coat. It was quite hard to unlock the fingers.

Now the drama of the theatre was gathering momentum. Mr Cope had entered in his usual silence, and stood in their midst with bowed head, holding out both hands for gloves. Hazel, Peter and the rest swarmed round the patient, making all ready. The swathed and masked figure advanced to the table, to the spot where towels had been laid around the white skin. It stopped, and pointed, without looking round, to a scalpel, which Sister at once placed in his gloved hand. The usual passes were made, but Peter, instead of watching, was counting the people in the room once more. His nerves again: this time it felt as if there were too few.

Then, while he counted, a shriek froze the air. Dr Banner was on his feet, staring. 'What's this?' he shouted. 'Stop him, quickly!' Hazel dropped the towel she was holding and grabbed the surgeon's wrist. At the same moment, Peter, not yet fully alive to what was being done, instinctively seized the gowned figure from behind.

All were too late. For some minutes they could only gaze in fascination at the scalpel, still quivering in the terrible wound. A dresser fell to the floor like a stone. It was left to Sister to do the obvious thing. She flung herself through the glass door, screaming these words:

'Murder! Murder! Come quick! Help! Mr Cope's mad! He's murdered the patient.'

As for Peter, he just stood clutching the empty gown, which had collapsed in his grasp, the empty gloves still in the sleeves, while cap and mask fluttered to the floor. He had no comment to make, and never would.

Out of the sluice and into this pandemonium strode a familiar figure, that of Montagu Cope, FRCS. His bearded jowls were quivering with annoyance.

'I was beginning to think my presence was not required,' he snapped. 'No one troubled to fetch me, and as our hospital joker had jammed my door again, I was delayed some time. When at length I got out, my cap and gown had vanished. Well – stop staring like that and lend a hand! What is the matter with you all? I'm operating here today . . .'

## HOMICIDAL MANIAC!

*Pamela Vincent*

The trees were much thicker here, often shutting out the moonlight in a sudden well of darkness.

They were her enemies, trees. She never did like woods, even in daytime, and at night she could imagine that the trees were ganging up on her, crowding together to swallow up her headlights as they swung from one side to the other along the winding road.

She hadn't expected to be so conscious of the loneliness. A fast run on empty roads was all very well, but there hadn't been another car in miles and it was barely midnight – what did they *do* with themselves in the country? Didn't anyone go out in the evening? She wondered now whether she'd been wise to refuse the offer of a bed: this was no place to break down, for sure.

She shuddered. A million evil things could happen here and no one would ever know. Still, only another hour and she'd be home.

The car lurched and immediately she knew the worst had happened. The last place anyone would choose to change a tyre, damn it!

Resignedly she wobbled to a halt and climbed out into a suddenly silent world, shivering in the night air. A self-reliant young woman, she was quite capable of changing a wheel, and the car was parked on the verge in a pool of moonlight that had somehow penetrated the leafy density, so there was nothing to stop her setting about the job as swiftly and efficiently as she did everything else. Nothing but the need to stare into the shadows and reassure herself that she was, indeed, as alone as she must certainly be.

Who could be here, miles from anywhere on a freezing night?

'Imagination,' she told herself. 'Everyone imagines he's being watched. It's a form of conceit!'

She kept her eyes on what she was doing, trying to hurry as her fingers chilled on icy metal, trying to become absorbed so that she could forget the hostile woods all around her and what they might conceal.

'For goodness' sake, woman! If there's a homicidal maniac about, he'd just pounce – he wouldn't wait around in the cold, watching you. Come to that, he wouldn't be waiting around anyway in the cold on the offchance that some girl on her own would have a puncture –'

She paused in what she was doing. She hadn't thought about what had caused the puncture. He could have put something on the road . . .

He?

She'd only just invented the homicidal maniac and already he was assuming a personality!

She looked around furtively.

No one.

Naturally.

'How'd he know who might run over whatever it was? He might have got a couple of hefty truck-drivers!'

Then he'd merely have lain low until they'd gone away, and set his trap for a later victim.

Despite her best intentions, her eyes strayed to the trees again. Queer shapes, uncannily still. She glanced across the road to the other side.

And the moon disappeared behind a cloud.

She smothered a scream, not sure whether one of the twisted trunks had moved, had taken another form. For a long moment she held her breath, until the world swam back into light.

A man was leaning against a tree. It wasn't imagination, she could see his head and broad shoulders, his folded arms. He looked comfortable, settled, as if he'd been there for hours and was prepared to remain there for further hours.

He didn't alter his position when she stopped to stare and she hesitated, still not sure whether someone was there or not. Could anyone stay so still, knowing she'd seen him?

He must have moved slightly after all, for his eyes caught the light and for an instant glowed with a strange green luminosity like a cat's.

She started and peered harder, trying to make out his shape and size. It was difficult to separate his outline from the tree trunk. There was a – what was it? – a shagginess about him, something not quite normal. His stillness wasn't normal, either. It was as if he'd chosen a vantage point from which to view a performance . . .

She choked on a giggle.

'And now, ladies and gentlemen, for my next trick I will demonstrate the gentle art of changing a wheel on a cold night while being watched by a homicidal maniac!'

But was she being watched? She just couldn't be certain at this distance.

What was he waiting for? Why didn't he say something, at least? There was something animal-like about this passivity – that was it! She'd become aware of a smell, a strong, wild beast smell.

'And what would a bear or a gorilla be doing in an English wood?' she asked herself, on the edge of hysteria.

Leaning against a tree watching her change a tyre. Obviously.

They couldn't go on like this, just looking at each other.

'You might give me a hand if you're so interested!' she shouted suddenly, her voice shockingly loud.

He stirred, changed his position, straightened himself.

She tensed, regretting the impulse that had made her stir things up. He was tall, huge. It must be the uncertain light, but he looked seven feet high and almost as broad.

He *was* shaggy! His green eyes gleamed again and she felt panic mounting within her. There were tales of unnatural animals that no one could catch. Some people thought they were left here by UFO's . . .

'Now you're really getting fanciful.'

She looked wildly up and down the empty road. Surely *someone* must be wanting to use this route; it couldn't remain as empty as this all night? Someone *must* come soon, mustn't they? A lorry – they travelled at night – or a doctor, always being called out at unearthly hours. Anyone, a drunken reveller, as long as he was human . . .

There was nowhere to run to, he could catch her easily on the road, and she couldn't plunge into the trees and undergrowth. Why had he left her alone so long? Did he enjoy this cat-and-mouse game, prolonging the suspense for both of them?

Desperately she turned back to try to finish the job before he attacked, keeping her eyes on his shadowy outline. Hadn't he moved over to a different tree, one that was nearer?

If only a car would come!

The animal smell seemed stronger and she peered suspiciously to see whether he was nearer still. So many trees to help him, against her.

At last! The faint noise of a car-engine, far away. Let it be on this road, coming this way! It simply must.

It did sound louder. She tried to remember whether she'd passed any turn-offs that might lead it away, but it *had* to stay on this road. It couldn't be so close and then leave her alone again with a maniac who was growing bolder. He'd moved again, no doubt about it, nearer still – hadn't he been by a tree with twin trunks before?

Headlights flared and hysterically she flung herself into the roadway, almost being run down as the driver swerved and braked.

'Please – please – help me –'

Sobbing with relief she stumbled towards the car, hardly aware of who was in it – it was just *people*, safety.

Both front doors opened and two men leapt out to catch her as she fell into their arms.

'I thought no one was ever coming – I didn't know what to do – I had a puncture –'

'What is it? What happened?' one of them spoke sharply, trying to stem the flow of words.

'A man – a thing – there, over there –'

She turned to point, but now there was no shaggy figure watching from the shadows. Not anywhere.

'He was there, by that tree!'

'What did he do? Did he hurt you?'

'No, he just stood there, watching me.'

'Are you sure? Moonlight plays funny tricks.'

'He was real! I saw him. He was creeping nearer all the time, dodging from tree to tree –'

'You said he was just standing there.'

'He was. He *was*! But then he'd move to another tree and stand still again, looking at me.' She shuddered. 'It was horrible.'

'Could you see what he looked like?'

'He was huge, and shaggy-looking, and his eyes glowed green –'

One of the men gave a bark of laughter.

'Glowing eyes!'

'They did glow. Like an animal's. There was a smell like an animal, too, a big animal, a bear or something.'

'Oh, so it was a bear, not a man?'

She was trembling and the other man took pity on her.

'She's had a bad fright,' he said. 'Whatever you saw, or thought you saw, Miss, it's gone now.'

He looked at his companion while he continued speaking to her.

'Your car'll be safe where it is. We'll pick it up in the morning.'

They put her between them in the front seat and soon they were turning off into a long drive leading to a darkened house.

'Won't we be disturbing someone?' she asked doubtfully, as they slammed doors and clattered up the steps.

'It's all right, there's no one here but us.'

They switched on the hall lights and gratefully she entered the warm interior, sinking into a deep armchair. She looked around.

And then she noticed the strange style of decoration – not what she had expected to find in a gracious country house. Pictures and sculptures that made her blink; objects in leather and metal whose use she could barely guess at; whips and chains – what would anyone want with all those things?

For the first time she was able to take a good look at her rescuers. They were grinning at each other.

'Now we can have a little fun, don't you think?' said one, turning with slow deliberation to put the chain on the front door.

It was an effort to drag her eyes away from his bony fingers and their unnaturally long nails as they completed the task of shutting out the world of normal midnight terrors. The other man was looking at her, his tongue moving slowly over lips dry with anticipation.

As their eyes met, he smiled, a secret smile filled with inner pleasure not to be shared, and his gaze flickered towards the Black Museum on the wall.

'Yes,' he agreed, 'I think we can.'

# MY VERY GOOD FRIEND

*Bernard Taylor*

There was no doubt about it, the insect had grown. Not only did it look larger, but Pierre could tell – holding it gently in the palm of his hand – that it was also heavier.

Studying the slender green creature, Pierre experienced a sensation of great pride and satisfaction. After all his months of research he was finally seeing results. At last there was something to show for all those hours spent bending over his workbench in his small – almost primitive – laboratory. His early failures – and there had been so many of them – counted for nothing now in the face of his success.

Briefly he let his mind stray back into the past, seeing the seemingly-endless succession of ill-fated creatures that had been the subjects for his experiments. There had been so many: the flies, the yellow-jackets, the bees, the mosquitoes. And all of them had failed the test – not one had survived more than a very short time.

So he had gone on, making changes here, alterations there. The drug he now used was quite different from the one he had started with.

And then, once the drug had been perfected, he had found the praying mantises. Like his earlier subjects, the first ones had succumbed, but the next one – and what a time that was! – had survived for many weeks after the initial treatment.

Now here he was with the fifth. And after seven weeks of continuous treatment it showed no signs of weakening or deterioration. On the contrary, it seemed positively to glow with health – if it was possible for such a very green creature to glow. The rate of its growth was accelerating day by day also, Pierre had noticed. He smiled; he had known that he could do it – would do it – eventually.

He replaced the praying mantis in the small, mesh-covered cage he had made for it, then watched as the insect devoured a bluebottle that had been provided for its lunch. When the meal was finished the creature turned its head and gazed at its captor with strange, unfathomable eyes. It was uncanny, that, Pierre thought, how it could actually swivel its head from side to side, unlike most other insects. But there, the praying mantis was an extraordinary creature altogether.

Pierre never tired of studying the insect. He found that he could sit for hours, gazing with rapt fascination, just staring at it. It was not known as a praying mantis for nothing, he observed; it even adopted its praying attitude whilst eating. Pierre found it the most enthralling of all his subjects and he looked upon it with a profoundly respectful air, completely caught up in its mystery.

It *was* a mystery to him, too. Coming from Paris to the backwoods of America he had never seen a praying mantis before. Consequently he had been intrigued by the small, delicate-looking creature from the moment when he had first seen one – sitting on a twig outside the laboratory. Mesmerized, he had watched as the insect had snatched a small aphid from a nearby leaf and quickly devoured it.

Now, however, the smaller insects were no longer sufficient to supply the nutritional needs of the swiftly-growing creature. Its diet now consisted of the larger species – flies, moths, butterflies, etc. From an approximate length of one and a half inches the praying mantis now measured well over three. Soon, Pierre reckoned, he'd be able actually to inject the growth-giving serum – instead of brushing it on the bodies of the insects that had been caught for the creature's food.

With a satisfied sigh, Pierre turned off the light over the cage and stepped outside on to the veranda of the small house. He looked out over acres of woodland – only one other house visible among the trees. The owner of that house, Royston Stevens, was the only human he saw from one week to another. Apart from the occasional visits from his American neighbour, Pierre was entirely alone.

But this was the way he wanted it. This was the way it suited him. Never a gregarious person, he had at once welcomed the solitude of this place; it had accepted him and he had embraced its silence, its aloneness, knowing instinctively that it was right for him. Here he was free from the inquisitive glances of strangers, the half-fascinated, half-shocked glances that would be thrown in his direction.

In the glass of the kitchen window he saw, for a second, the image of his own reflection. It gazed back at him, a slight, deformed figure with stunted legs and distorted features. His face had something of the appearance of a clay model, one side of which had been forcibly dragged down in a fit of sudden anger. The face was ugly – shocking even to Pierre himself who had grown up with it. Only the eyes were beautiful. Soft, limpid, infinitely kind and gentle they shone, a clear, deep blue, twin oases in the desert of his ugliness.

Quickly he turned his head away – he could never look at himself for long.

When Royston Stevens visited the house a week later he found Pierre in the back yard hard at work on the construction of a large cage which he was covering with a coarse wire mesh. After their initial greetings Stevens asked:

'What's it for?'

For a long moment Pierre just looked at him, inwardly debating whether or not to impart the details of his wonderful secret. In the end he beckoned and led the way into his laboratory.

'There. Look,' he said proudly in his French-accented English.

Stevens looked towards the smaller cage on the work-bench and gasped.

'But . . . What is it?'

Pierre smiled – he couldn't help himself. 'What does it look like?' he asked in return.

'It's – it's like an enormous – praying mantis . . . !'

Pierre nodded. 'True.'

'Jesus . . . !' Stevens moved nearer to the cage, gazing in a kind of sick fascination at the huge insect before him.

'I call him Emil,' Pierre said, grinning widely.

The mantis was now well over a foot in length and would clearly very soon be too large for the confines of its present home. The body of the insect was a brilliant green with a bright sheen on the skin. It sat there, as always, its short, powerful forearms held together in their attitude of prayer.

'How . . . ?' was all that Stevens managed to say.

Later, over coffee, Pierre related the story of his experiments.

'Don't you realize what this will mean to the world?' Pierre asked excitedly. 'Do you realize that humanity need never hunger again?'

Looking at the ugly face before him, the American silently framed the question: Why are you so concerned for humanity when you can't even *face* humanity? And anyway, what has it ever done for you . . . ? Then, concentrating on the soft blue eyes, he said aloud:

'It's wonderful, Pierre. Wonderful.'

Later they looked again at Emil.

'I can see why you're building a bigger cage,' Stevens said.

'Yes. Emil must have room to move around. He must be comfortable.'

'Why "Emil"?'

The Frenchman shrugged. 'I used to have a dog. He was Emil.'

'How do you know this one's male, anyway?'

'I don't. But does it matter?' Pierre laughed suddenly. 'If I find he is a lady I shall change her name. To Emilie.'

And so Emil grew. Two weeks later Pierre moved the insect into the larger cage which had been placed on the veranda.

The praying mantis now measured over three feet in height, and the drug for its growth was administered directly by injection. Perhaps he should stop giving the drug, Pierre thought, but no, he couldn't. Having seen his experiment working so successfully he felt compelled, somehow, to continue.

Pierre never tired of gazing at his pet (he had ceased to think of Emil merely as the subject of an experiment), and he spent many long hours sitting or standing before the cage, observing the enormous creature within. At his approach, Pierre would see the large, intelligent-looking head turn to watch him. The eyes that looked into his own were filled with trust.

Feeding times were a source of endless fascination. Pierre had taken now to trapping birds and then releasing them into the confines of the cage. The praying mantis would turn its head, attracted by the frantic fluttering, the keen eyes watching, studying as the terrified bird sought a means of escape. Apart from the slow, measured movement of the head, Emil's body would be quite still, absolutely motionless. Carefully the insect seemed to be judging the distance between itself and its prey. And then, suddenly, without warning, Emil would go into action. The forelegs would shoot out – so swiftly that their movement was, to Pierre's eyes, just a blur – and the unsuspecting bird would be snatched up, caught in the strong, unrelenting grasp, and carried to the large waiting jaws.

Pierre always looked away at this point. He found it impossible to watch as the birds were devoured. The fact that the birds were killed at all brought him considerable distress but, he reasoned with himself, it was necessary.

With Pierre, Emil was gentleness itself. Quite without fear the Frenchman could go right into the cage. There he would stand, talking to his pet, whispering his soft, soothing words. He would stroke the neck of the large green creature, and the trusting eyes would watch him, following his every move.

Pierre found that, within himself, a great fondness, a great love, was growing for his pet. There was a rapport here that he had never experienced before.

As time went on Emil began to wait anxiously for Pierre's coming. Seeing him approach the bars of the cage the insect would hurry towards him, tiny piercing cries issuing from its wide mouth. Pierre, hearing the sounds, seeing the eagerness, would feel his heart leap with joy and affection. Here was a living creature who never noticed his deformities. The eyes of the praying mantis never flinched when they lighted on its jailer. Instead they studied him with a fondness akin to his own. It was a mutual love and trust, and Pierre gloried in it.

'What happened to your insect friend?'

Royston Stevens sat opposite Pierre over their coffee cups. There had been no mention of Emil since the American's arrival some fifteen minutes before, and he was burning with curiosity.

Pierre smiled. It had been some weeks since the two men had last met and he was quite sure that Stevens had not visited him merely for his coffee – good though it was.

'Come. I will show you.' Still smiling, Pierre arose and led the way on to the back porch. There, inside the cage, was the praying mantis.

'My God!' Stevens cried, aghast. He stared open-mouthed at the enormous creature that crouched there and turned its head to study him with cool, impassioned eyes.

'It's . . . it's grotesque!'

'No. No.' Pierre frowned momentarily, then murmuring, 'Beautiful, beautiful,' he moved to the cage and thrust an arm through between the bars.

'Emil . . . Emil.' He crooned the name softly, seductively, and Stevens watched as the huge praying mantis moved eagerly towards the outstretched hand.

'You see?' Pierre asked the gaping American. 'There is nothing grotesque. Grotesque? How can you say such a thing?' He began to stroke the creature's head. Emil revelled in the sensation.

'How can you bear to touch it?' Stevens asked. 'Aren't you afraid?'

Afraid? Pierre laughed at the idea. 'He's tame,' he said. 'Can't you see? We understand one another.' He saw the look of horrified doubt on the American's face, then added:

'Watch.'

Slipping up the catch, Pierre pushed open the door and went inside. Stevens moved closer, watching intently.

'Emil is my very good friend,' Pierre said, smiling through the bars, his bright blue eyes crinkling. 'My very, very good friend.'

Stevens said nothing, and Pierre went on:

'Our relationship is based on mutual trust and love. Emil trusts me. Emil loves me.'

Stevens forced himself to try to relax. He tried a smile in return. 'I'm sure you're right,' he said. 'But you must admit it's bound to give anyone a bit of a shock.'

'Ah, yes, of course. But that's because you don't know Emil.'

He reached out and ran one gentle caressing hand down the long green length of the insect's body. Under his touch Emil gave a small shudder of delight and moved closer to him.

Pierre continued to stroke his friend and after a few moments Emil's head began to turn slowly from side to side – left to right – right to left, giving the creature the appearance of a huge green puppet.

'I think perhaps you are female after all,' Pierre chuckled, smoothing the bright skin. 'I think perhaps I should have called you Emilie.' His hand moved faster now, like butterflies on the sensitive body, fluttering, titillating, and Emil's head moved quicker in response.

Stevens, watching in fascination, saw the enormous creature give a tremendous wriggle of joy. There was something incredibly obscene and disgusting about the spectacle before him, yet he found it impossible to look away. He gazed enthralled as the praying mantis – easily a foot taller than Pierre – throbbed and pulsated to the touch of the Frenchman's hand.

'Pierre . . . Pierre,' he said, 'I think you should come out.'

'Nonsense!' Pierre answered, laughing. 'Emil – *Emilie* is enjoying herself!'

The whole body of the praying mantis seemed to be quivering now in an ecstasy of sensual delight. Stevens saw the creature's form arch then straighten, then arch again, and he knew quite suddenly, beyond any shadow of doubt, that the insect was indeed female. And just as certainly he knew that the innocent, unknowing Pierre was more to her than just a very good friend.

The movements of the creature now became more frantic, taking on the aspect of some ancient, ritualistic dance. And suddenly Pierre became afraid.

With his own realization of the sex of his captive he saw the weird gyrations in a new light – the praying mantis was doing some kind of mating dance. Memory flooded back to him of things read – things he had thought were forgotten. He gave a terrified scream and backed away towards the door of the cage.

Emilie followed him, reaching out for him, clasping him to her. Then, held in her powerful embrace, he felt a gigantic shudder shake the huge green form. Pierre gave a great wrench and, with a strength born of desperation, made another lurch for the door. Even though he reached it, however, there was no room for him to open it inwards. He screamed again, his bright blue eyes starting from their sockets in his abject terror as he gazed at Stevens, beseeching his help.

But there was no time. Even as Stevens looked about him for something with which to ward off the attack, Emilie moved in again.

Pierre fought desperately but in another moment his great lover was upon him. Her two short, immensely-powerful arms snapped out and clutched him to her.

Emilie was just behaving true to her instincts.

Held immovable in her deathly sweetheart's embrace, Pierre gave one last scream. Then, with a short, swift movement, Emilie's jaws descended, yawning, gaping above him. He tried to scream again but the mouth, hard, horny on his flesh, had clamped over his face, stopping all further sound.

Emilie's eyes never lost their look of love as she wrenched off his head.

# AND NOW THE PACT

*Martin Ricketts*

Browsing among the dusty bookcases of an old second-hand shop, Miller found the worn leather-bound tome jammed behind a shelf. He flicked its faded yellow pages curiously, at length realizing that he was leafing through an ancient volume of magic spells. He laughed, then frowned as a certain heading caught his attention: BEING AN INSTRUCTION FOR SUMMONING THE DEVIL OR AN ASSISTANT THEREOF. He snorted and slapped the book shut. But he did not put it back on the shelf; instead, some odd subliminal instinct made him buy it. Then, clutching it to him as if it were a child, he took it home.

When he drew the star on his cellar floor he didn't really expect anything to happen. Feeling foolish, he chalked in the outer-circle and then the inner, then put candles on all the places where the points of the star touched the circles. He opened the old book at the appropriate page and recited the spell.

Instantly the lamp that hung from the ceiling smashed in its socket and the room was plunged into darkness, save for the flickering light from the candles. The temperature dropped noticeably and Miller, in his shirt-sleeves, began to shiver with the cold. He felt suddenly frightened. Then, eyes focusing with difficulty in the dirty light, he stared. There, in the air above the middle of the inner-circle, a curious threatening shape was slowly materializing.

Miller stepped backwards, flattened himself against the wall. He gaped, transfixed, as the shape became more and more distinct. Finally it was completely recognizable. Then he knew; his experiment had worked! There was no mistaking those horns, that peculiar pointed tail or those tiny leather bat-wings.

'You want to make a pact?' the demon asked.

Miller swallowed. 'I . . . um, I . . .'

The demon stepped out of the diagram and came closer to Miller, who flinched away from the rotten smell.

'Well?'

Miller nodded slowly. 'Well . . . I . . . I suppose I do . . .'

The demon smiled. 'All right. What is it you want? Money?

Fast cars? Women?'

Miller's tongue darted along his lips. Eager thoughts were suddenly beginning to trickle through his brain. 'Yeah, yeah,' he said quickly. 'All those . . .'

'Yes, they all do.' The demon leered. 'You realize, of course, the price you will have to pay for all this?'

Miller nodded.

'All right,' said the demon. 'Money first . . .'

Miller jumped in fright as chunks of yellow metal materialized in the middle of the room, flashing and flickering suddenly in the cold light, and thudding down to lie in gleaming heaps across the floor.

Miller gaped incredulously. 'Gold?' he whispered.

'Gold,' confirmed the demon.

Unbelieving, Miller bent down to pick up a piece of the shining metal, but it was much too heavy. 'You said I was to have money,' he complained at last.

The demon inclined its head. 'You're a foolish man. This is much better than normal currency: you can get rid of it anywhere, no questions asked, and it *never* loses its value.'

Miller nodded, eyes widening as the logic clicked home. 'Yeah, yeah. Now the fast cars – that was next, wasn't it?'

'Look out in your driveway,' the demon said.

Miller stood for a moment as if paralysed, looking uncertain. Then, galvanized suddenly into action, he leapt up the steps from the cellar and ran to his front door. In the driveway were a black Lotus Elan, a gleaming red Marcos and an ice-blue Mercedes.

He stood back from the door and closed his eyes. His heart was pounding like a runaway hammer-press. It's a dream, he thought, that's all it is. None of this is true. In a moment I'll look out in the driveway and those cars will be gone; I'll go down into the cellar and there'll be nothing there but my candles and chalk-marks on the floor. He opened his eyes and was vaguely startled by the gloominess of the hallway. Slowly he looked round the open door. The cars were still there.

Laughing, he pounded back down the steps to the cellar. The demon grinned at him. The pile of gold was still there; and beside it was a girl – blonde, beautifully proportioned and completely nude.

Miller stopped abruptly at the bottom of the steps. He gaped;

in his throat was a lump which he unsuccessfully tried to swallow.

'. . . and women!' finished the demon.

'I . . . I . . .' Miller drooled. He could hardly believe what he saw. Her eyes were deep and dark, gazing at him seductively and pleasurably; her figure was soft and rounded, skin as smooth as cream and the colour of ivory. Miller's hands felt hot and clammy.

'What do I have to do?' he said eagerly. 'Where do I have to sign?'

'You don't sign anywhere,' the demon told him. 'All you have to do is say: "In return for services rendered I agree to sell my soul to the devil."'

'And if I don't?'

The demon waved its arm in a tiny sweeping gesture. 'Then you'll lose all this. And you'll have – excuse the pun – you'll have the devil of a job getting rid of me now that you've called me up; I'll pester you day and night for the rest of your life. You won't have a moment's rest.'

Miller nodded slowly. 'All right.'

'You agree?'

'Yes.'

'Then say it.'

'All right.' Miller paused. He glanced around uncertainly. Then suddenly, making up his mind, he blurted: 'In return for services rendered I agree to sell my soul to the devil.'

The demon's face relaxed into a grin, a yellow-toothed, malevolent-eyed rictus of evil delight. 'There, that didn't hurt, did it? Enjoy yourself – while you can.' It gave a little bow, then abruptly vanished.

The girl stepped round the pile of gold and came towards Miller. She was just a few inches shorter than he was, and smelling of some exquisite perfume. He took a self-conscious step backwards, acutely aware of the stubble on his chin, his grubby shirt and his torn, muddied trousers. But the girl didn't seem to notice; her eyes gazed steadily into his. She smiled and held out a slender hand towards him.

'Where is your bedroom, Mr Miller?'

As if in a trance, Miller took the proffered hand – it was warm and smooth – and led her up the steps out of the cellar. Without a word they walked through the dark silence of the house, up the stairs and into the dismal untidiness of his bedroom. Now he was breathing faster. Her warmth and fragrance and incredibly intangible sexiness were doing things to his stomach. A tiny half-growl forced itself up from his throat and out between his parted teeth. He turned and grabbed her and threw her down on to the unmade bed. She seemed oblivious of the roughness with which he handled her; she lay on the bed submissively, ready to please, eyes sensuously closed. Miller was on top of her before he was completely undressed, his thick hard lips seeking the voluptuous softness of her neck and shoulders.

Then abruptly she vanished.

Miller twisted, suddenly perplexed to find himself caressing nothing but wrinkled bedclothes. 'Wha – ?' He sat up on the bed, legs tangled awkwardly in his trousers.

'Come along, Miller,' the demon said.

'Uh?' Miller's head jerked sideways to stare at the scarlet figure perched on the foot-board of his bed.

'But . . . What . . . ? I . . .'

'Come on, Miller,' the demon repeated. 'You've sold yourself to us. Now I've come to *take* you!'

Miller blinked. 'What's happening? The girl – where is she?'

'Never mind about that. She was just bait for the fish.'

'Fish?'

'Yes, Miller.' The demon looked at him and sneered. 'You! *You're* the fish!'

'But our agreement! You're supposed to wait until I'm dead! I'm supposed to live my life to the full, any way I want. *Then* you take me!'

The demon grinned. '*That's* not what we agreed. You've been listening to too many stories. You shouldn't believe all those old legends, you know – none of them are true . . .'

Miller quivered. 'But we made a deal!' he protested. 'This is totally dishonest! What about those "services rendered" that I haven't had?'

The demon shook its head sadly. 'You didn't really expect honesty from *us*, did you?'

Miller yelped and tried to stand, but the trousers wrapped round his ankles brought him crashing down on to the floor. He rolled over, screamed, then crossed his arms in front of his face. His bedroom was suddenly blurring and fragmenting around him. A huge pit seemed to open beneath him. Flames icked out, leaping towards him like oily serpents. Heat wafted ıp, searing his legs. Then suddenly he was falling, dropping lown into the fiery mouth that opened like a bright wound o receive him.

Then he was gone. In the darkened bedroom the demon :xecuted a neat little pirouette, then disappeared. A peculiar mell of charred flesh, mingled with some other nameless odour, ingered momentarily on the air like the echo of some old ınd forgotten melody. Then, a second later, that too had lisappeared.

## THE HORROR UNDER PENMIRE

*Adrian Cole*

'enmire is strewn across the edge of one of the bleakest tretches of Cornish moorland in existence. Though the windwept houses are exposed constantly to the buffets of Atlantic ales, the withdrawn inhabitants live their lives in sheltered eclusion, rarely venturing beyond the proximities of their solated haven. There are few trees in Penmire, or indeed for niles around on this spectral, misted countryside – the hard utcrops of granite permit only the barest growths of gorse nd heather. Any who chance to pass this way would wonder ow it is that the villagers live.

Yet it has been thus for years without number. In its long, nchronicled history, Penmire has tenanted miners, farmers, ven smugglers from the secret coves of the not-too-distant oasts, where even today the caves and blow-holes shelter idden secrets. There have always been people here in Penmire, erhaps from the dawn of man; sometimes it is whispered broad on shadowed evenings that men worshipped at strange ltars in the marshes behind the village, and some folks hold hat Arthur took refuge here at one time, pursued across the noors by some hideous foe.

Only the tors of frowning granite know how long Penmire as stood, but the magic of distant ages still hangs wraith-like ver the quaint dwellings, suggesting primal antiquity and forgotten knowledge. What scenes of ancient savagery did th imperturbable moon gaze down upon through ragged, storm rent clouds? What dark arts were practised, what Neolithi sounds mingled with the roaring winds, to be torn and hurle across miles of barren wasteland?

Now the village seems to slumber, oblivious to the outsid world, contemplating, perhaps, its fabled past.

Roy Baxter had long been fascinated by the lure of mysti Penmire. He was a hard-working engineer from Bristol, o 'up-country' as the locals termed it, but his hobby was thi deep interest in folklore and mythology. It was a hobby whic led him all over England, pottering around on ancient sites and browsing through musty, faded records.

He was on holiday now, driving fairly aimlessly through th enchanting hamlets of Cornwall, the county that perhaps drev him most, and it was here in the tiny pubs that he first hear muted comments about Penmire. It was just the sort o guarded half-secret that he looked for, but no one was anxiou to locate the place for him. His curiosity was fully aroused – he often found the local people non-committal concerning th old legends, despite their talkative natures – but an unnatura barrier of silence would always clamp down the moment h tried to bring Penmire into the conversation. In one little pu he saw a group of farmers down pints and fairly rush out int the night, though he may have imagined their rapid exit.

Baxter's fertile imagination worked further overtime whe he tried to pinpoint Penmire on a map. All his efforts faile There simply weren't any records of the place anywhere, o Ordnance Survey maps or local records.

Despite this disappointment, Baxter was thrilled. He wa certain that the village existed and determined all the more t find it. Acting on the assumption from what little he ha heard, that Penmire was somewhere on the central moorland he tried to cover as much of that foreboding landscape as h could, but it was a fruitless task. Thick fingers of fog obscure the hidden paths and narrow roadways that could have le him there. Infuriated, he came off the moors and drove int Bodmin, where he checked into a small hotel.

That evening he came down the creaking stairs, duckin under a thick beam, and came into the foyer.

'May I use the phone?' he asked his dumpy, rosy-cheeke hostess. She was a cheerful soul, ample-bosomed and bounc typical of the loquacious landlady.

''Course you can, Mr Baxter,' she chirped in a high voice, elongating her R's in the curious Cornish fashion.

'Fine. I want to call London, actually.'

'Oh, that's all right. Business, I s'pose?' Mrs Harcott was all smiles. She was already imagining Baxter to be a big-time executive or possibly a TV producer. Her gossip circles would shortly be afire with the news.

'Yes,' Baxter grinned, thinking it would all go on the bill anyway. 'Oh, by the way,' he added, trying to sound casual, 'uh, I noticed a turning on the moor for a place called – what was it? – ah, Penmire. Yes, that was it, Penmire. It seems I've heard of it in local customs and the like. Only I'm rather keen on that sort of thing. Do you know the place at all?' He had lied about that turn-off, but he wanted to see if Mrs Harcott would deny all knowledge of Penmire. Her mouth was slightly open, as though he had taken her by surprise. She began idly flicking through her guest-book, and Baxter knew he had found another peculiar link in the mysterious armour of that moorland village.

'Well, I 'ave 'eard of it, Mr Baxter, but I can't say as I know where 'tis. I 'spect you'd find out in the bar tonight, though. We do 'ave some of the local landowners in 'ere sometimes. But if 'tis on the moors, I'd keep away if I were you, Mr Baxter. 'Tis awful bleak up there, 'specially with the mist.'

'I see. Well, thanks anyway, Mrs Harcott. Perhaps you're right.' That was all he'd get out of her. So the place did exist.

'You're welcome,' she returned, but her air of pleasantness had dissipated. Baxter found the phone tucked away in a convenient niche, and after a series of brief interchanges eventually got through to a London number.

'Hallo, Phil? This is Roy.' There was a pause before he heard the voice of his life-long friend.

'Hallo, there. Long time no see. What have you been doing with yourself? Are you at home?' Philip Dayton's voice was warm, firm, painting a picture of a strong character.

'No, I'm in Cornwall, actually.'

'Ah, the legend-haunted south-west,' Dayton chuckled. He was more than familiar with his friend's obsession with mythology. Himself an expert in the field, he guessed the reason for this call at once. Roy was 'on to something'. Dayton grinned to himself as he thought of some of the ridiculous 'finds' his pal had unearthed in the last few years.

'Yes,' said Baxter. 'I've got a few weeks off to pursue my true calling as usual.'

'Very nice. And what have you dug up from the pixie-infested tin mines this time?'

'Well, nothing as yet. But I've come across an interesting case.'

'Oh?' Dayton was intrigued by his friend's tone, for, despite Baxter's ability to stumble across events of absolutely no importance whatsoever, he did occasionally find something interesting.

'Ever heard of Penmire?'

'Penmire? No, can't place it offhand.'

'It's a small village on Bodmin Moor, but I don't know where. If you can't direct me to it, no one can.' Baxter sounded urgent. He knew Philip Dayton's knowledge of legend and folklore was extensive; Dayton had written several authoritative books on the subject, and had read as much material as he could find.

'Ah, Penmire. It does ring the faintest of bells. Vaguely connected with Arthur, and with a history of Druidic dabblings to boot. Yes, I know of it, though I can't tell you the gory details until I've dredged them up.'

'Well, it's a start,' exclaimed Baxter. 'Where the blue blazes is the place?'

'That I don't know. In fact I think you're in a blind alley, old sport. As far as I remember the place is only legendary anyway. A bit like the evasive Camelot.'

'Oh no!' Baxter groaned. 'Don't tell me it doesn't exist!'

'I'm not sure. I'm not too well up in those channels. Tell you what, though.'

'Uh-huh?'

'Where are you exactly?'

Baxter gave his address and his friend took it down.

'Bodmin, eh? Right. You hang on down there, and perhaps have a scout round for our hidden Penmire. In the meantime I'll see what I can find out about it at this end, then I might just drive down and join you.'

'You needn't do that, Phil, thanks all the same. I don't want to drag you off on a wild-goose chase.'

There was a laugh from the other end of the line. 'Nonsense I'm hooked. Matter of fact I'm at a loose end at the moment

I've just finished a series of University lectures, and I had thought about going up to the Yorkshire Moors for a spot of research. Witches and all that. But I must admit Bodmin Moor sounds just as enterprising.'

'Working on a new book?'

'Yup. Haven't done a damn thing yet, though. So your little find might furnish me with a few new tidbits. I could do with a break, and I haven't drunk a few jars with you for some time.'

'Great. In that case I'll stick around. When will you be here?'

'Oh, say three days. I should be able to ferret something out by then.'

'Right. Give my love to Annie and the kids.' Baxter rang off.

Philip Dayton scratched his head irritably and sipped his scotch, his thoughts running back once more to the events of the last few days. Where the hell was Roy? Five days ago he'd phoned him, enthusing about Penmire and its superstitious connotations. Two days ago, he, Dayton, had arrived here in Bodmin with enough information to help find the place, but Roy was nowhere to be found. That just wasn't like him.

Dayton now sat in the cramped bar of his friend's hotel, where he too had checked in. No one had been able to help. Mrs Harcott had seen Roy leave shortly after phoning him, and his few things were still in his room; she hadn't seen him since. Dayton had made several abortive attempts to eke information out of the people who used the bar, but he got the same shrugs from all of them. Hardly anyone had seen him, anyway, as he'd left the hotel shortly after checking in.

Dayton got little sleep that night; he began to get progressively more worried. His eyes turned again and again to the monolith on the hill above Bodmin, which stood out clearly against the purple skies. He turned this way and that in a restless half-slumber, while the brass pixies on the mantelpiece seemed to contort themselves into weird shapes. In the early hours of the morning, Dayton settled on a plan of action: he couldn't hang around lamely any longer. Roy must have found Penmire, otherwise he would have been back.

After a hurried breakfast, Dayton drove up on to Bodmin Moor and began searching the hedgeless side-roads and lesser tracks, from time to time consulting a rough map he had improvised in the records section of a London library. He pulled up at the base of a chain of huge, jutting tors, crowned with bare outcrops of wind-swept rock. According to his information, Penmire should be on the other side. There was an old road somewhere, but the chances were that it would be overgrown and hard to find.

Dayton got out, locking the car, and began the steep climb, his feet sinking slightly into the moss that dotted these lowest slopes. It was a gorgeous day; for once the sky was free of clouds and the sun beat down, giving the usually foreboding landscape a more welcoming quality. It was July, typically hot and windless. He could hear the skylarks twittering incessantly, though they were too high up to be seen against the glare. As he climbed he felt fresh and alive, at one with the land. His doubts about Roy dispersed in the joy of the climb.

As he reached the rock sentinels atop the tor, Dayton let out a deep sigh, mopped his brow and looked back at the clear vista below him. Far off he saw the sun glinting on the metal of speeding cars as they raced down the main road. You're missing it all, he thought. After a moment he turned and clambered through the dark rocks which were splotched here and there with thin patches of lichen. Once he'd crossed the top of the tor, he looked down with a satisfied grunt at the straggling houses below.

Unless I miss my guess, that'll be Penmire – picturesque little spot, he mused. A sparkling stream ran out of the distant village, twisting its way into the limits of his vision, where a dark mass of trees formed a wood at the edge of the moors. Beyond Penmire lay the marshes, a flattish area, peppered with bogs and mires, which the old records had mentioned, and behind them rose a series of rugged tors, leading off hazily into the heart of the moorland.

Dayton was about to start the descent, when he heard muffled voices somewhere behind him. At least, he thought they had come from behind him. He turned, half expecting to see a basking courting couple, but his gaze encountered only the blank rocks. Damn fool, he said to himself. On a day like this voices carry a long way.

He took off his jacket, slung it unceremoniously over his shoulder and began to climb down into the broad valley. He hadn't noticed it, but the skylarks were no longer audible. Looking down on Penmire, he could see that it was oddly lifeless, as though it had been long abandoned. That was strange, because according to Dayton's information it should be populated. Still, he was some way off yet, though he couldn't see any vehicles or telephone wires. To all intents and purposes the place was dead.

As he pressed on, expecting to see at least a sheep or two, Dayton was suddenly aware of the silence, broken only by his passage through the tufts of reed. He stood still and realized just how absurdly quiet it was. He was reminded of Alice stepping through the looking glass. *So where is the white rabbit?* He felt eyes on him too, though he had to suppress a chuckle at his own nerves. Perhaps the villagers had seen him approach – in a place as remote as this they wouldn't appreciate strangers. But he should have been able to hear the birds or at least the teeming insect life: the grasshoppers and crickets usually made a terrific din.

Behind him, towering up into the sunlight, the rocks seemed to leer down mockingly. Dayton shrugged and moved on. Roy's car should be around somewhere, he told himself. He'd feel a lot easier when he saw it. He heard the faintest suggestions of voices again and cursed himself; he put it down to exertion – after all, he was not a young man. Penmire was still some way off when he noticed a sudden chill in the air. The psychical research boys would love this place. Then he laughed inwardly as he saw the reason for the drop in temperature.

Coming across the brow of a nearby tor was a thick mist, lapping over the rocks and overspilling into the valley. These moor mists can be frightening to those who don't know them – they appear from almost nowhere and literally descend like blankets in a matter of minutes. Dayton had tramped Dartmoor to the east, and knew how quickly he would be enveloped by those swirling, silent tendrils.

He speeded up his descent, certain now that he could hear those indefinable voices. It was uncanny, made even more so by this thickening mist. The stuff seemed to tremble with animation as it reached out and engulfed him. Dayton calculated that he had about a mile to go. He stumbled on, muttering obscenities, through the gathering coils.

There then burst on his ears a chorus of sounds that stopped him dead in his tracks. He was in the heart of the mist when, as if at a given signal, thousands of frogs burst into voice, the sound of their deep croaking coming from all around the valley. Dayton reflected that it was the most chilling sound he had ever heard. He tried to see into the mist, but out of all those countless frogs he could see none. He was scared, no use in pretending otherwise, but he smiled grimly. The mist had probably alarmed them. Sitting at home in an armchair was one thing, but when you were alone in this lot it was a different matter.

Far off he heard a splashing vaguely over the cacophony of frogs. That would be the stream, etching its way through the boulders. But this was too rhythmic for a stream, more as though someone were sloshing their way through water or mud. An inhabitant at last? Dayton thought of shouting, but the sound appeared to recede, and, for some unaccountable reason, he thought it had gone *underground*. But so many odd things had occurred already that he cursed himself and carried on.

Abruptly the frogs were silent, and the abysmal silence supplanted their terrible racket. Dayton barked his shins more than once, now only vaguely certain of the direction in which Penmire lay. His progress had become far more difficult, for he had to skirt sinking clods of peat and slime-covered pools of mire. He was sweating profusely, his face damp with mist. Where was that blasted village? He leant on a huge granite slab and wheezed. *Roy, my son, heads shall roll for this.*

The events of the next few seconds were a total shock to him, and concrete proof that something was very much amiss with this weird valley. The rock on which he was leaning seemed to twitch, as the flank of a horse twitches when irritated by a fly. Dayton drew back in horrified alarm, half expecting something dark and malign to rear up out of the mire. Then the earth heaved, and he pitched forward into the soaking reeds. 'This is ridiculous!' he kept saying, over and over again, but the ground *rippled* as though it were water, and Dayton bit off a scream.

It must be an island of turf, he told himself desperately, for anything else would be far too alien to accept. He struggled to his feet and ran, though it was like standing in a small boat. He stumbled again before the movements stopped, then rushed on as far as the reeds and hidden rocks would allow. This time he could definitely hear voices, though they seemed as much inside of him as out in those sentient mists. The voices laughed, chuckling insanely at his plight: voices which he knew instinctively were not human.

The mist was now as thick as the fogs that he knew in London. God, how far away all that was. On and on he wandered, his shins bruised and bleeding from innumerable bumps on the hard granite that lay obscured everywhere he turned. A rumbling like distant thunder caught his attention, coming from the marsh, and again it seemed to come from *under* the earth. But that was unthinkable.

Dayton's progress had slowed right down, his breath coming in laboured gasps. The mist was playing tricks, though the sound had receded. Now all he could hear was the drip, drip of moisture on the reeds, faint though that sound was. Something dark and suggestive loomed up ahead, and he fell to his knees, heart pounding like a locomotive. *God, this is it.*

But it was only a house. He had reached the sanctuary of Penmire at last.

Painfully he limped between two houses, their eaves overhanging the path, their windows dark and shadowed. As he came into the street, he still had no idea where to start looking for Roy, assuming he was here. It was a relief to get off the marsh. Something stirred in the mist, and he recoiled in surprise. The skulking shape of a cat slunk past, eyes blazing with green hate, eyes that never left his own.

*Where is everyone?* Still the dense mist showed no signs of lifting. Dayton stumbled on up the badly-kept street, hands thrust deep in his pockets, numb with the cold, jacket pulled tight around him. He was conscious now of other cat-like shapes padding around the edge of his vision, but they were always obscured by the mist. At last he saw a dim light, and, coming upon what appeared to be an old inn, he pushed the thick wooden door and went inside.

Hostile eyes regarded him from at least five places as he closed the door. A bar ran the length of the far wall, while several tables were placed here and there around the little room. The walls were fitted with panelled cubicles, and nailed to the roof beams were brass horse-accoutrements, though Dayton couldn't see any horseshoes. He wasn't surprised.

An old woman sat at one of the tables, arms resting on a gnarled stick, a battered bag on the floor beside her slippered feet. Two weatherbeaten men sat in one of the chipped cubicles in the corner, smoking and playing cards. The barman, a huge, shirt-sleeved character with a pink, freckled face and thinning, sandy hair, was talking to what appeared to be a local labourer. There was thick mud on his boots. The barman scowled at Dayton as he came forward.

'We aren't open yet,' he said gruffly in a very strong accent. Dayton noticed a grubby collie lying at the labourer's feet, regarding him disdainfully.

'That's all right. Only I, uh, lost my way in this ruddy mist. It's a bit marshy out there and I don't fancy trying to find my way back to the car until the mist lifts.' The old lady regarded him through her spectacles, but never blinked. She might have been carved from granite for all she moved. No one spoke. Dayton edged nearer the bar, wary of the dog. Its owner had turned to inspect him, his gaze as scathing as his animal's. The card players had stopped.

'I don't suppose you've a phone . . .'

'No. There b'ain't none in Penmire,' returned the barman, taking a rag and wiping down the bar slowly and methodically.

'Oh. Well, I'm in a bit of a mess. Is there anywhere I can clean up?' The eyes stared questioningly. Christ, thought Dayton, what are they – zombies?

'From outside, be 'ee?' muttered the old girl beside him.

'Yes, that's right. London. I'm, er, looking for a friend of mine. I believe he's staying in Penmire.'

The woman nodded vaguely.

'I thought 'ee was from outside.'

'Hush, Mrs Dinnock,' muttered the barman. 'I think you're mistaken, sir. No one don't come to stay in Penmire.'

'Oh, but my friend expressly stated that he would be here.' Dayton watched the thick pipe-smoke curling up into the beams from the corner.

'No, I don't think so. No one has come. Only you.' Dayton shifted his gaze to the card players. They sat as though paralysed. What if Roy hadn't come here?

'Perhaps he'll turn up later. In the meantime, have you a gents handy? I must try and clean up a bit.'

'Through there,' grunted the barman reluctantly, pointing to a side door. Dayton nodded his thanks and went through. He found a tiny toilet and closed the flaking door behind him. There was an overpowering smell of fish exuding from the drain. Now what? he asked himself as he cleaned himself up in the battered sink. I was better off in the ruddy marsh.

He returned to the bar to find it empty, save for the inhospitable barman, who tried his damndest to ignore him.

'You get this mist often?'

'Ah.'

Dayton decided it was an affirmative. 'Like pea soup, eh?' he grinned, but it had no effect. Now I know how the lepers used to feel, he mused. 'Any chance of me buying a bite to eat?'

'Don't serve meals, sir. There's a shop down the street.'

'Hm. I'll hang on here till the mist lifts, I think. You, er, don't mind?' You hadn't better, he added to himself.

'May be down for a week. Often stops longer in the warm weather. My advice is to take the road off the moor, sir. You'll be all right. Folks in Penmire is wary of strangers.' The barman was fiddling about with glasses and glimpsing at a paper, anything to avoid being drawn into conversation.

'So I noticed. You, uh, sure about that friend of mine?'

'Positive.'

'O.K.' Dayton went over to one of the booths and sat down, pretending to study a map that he carried. The barman eyed him coldly and began cleaning glasses again. Outside everything remained silent.

Dayton had been seated for only a short time, when he noticed a book of some description poking up from the back of the seat opposite. Gently he reached over, careful not to be seen by the barman who had for a moment turned to his shelves, and picked it up. It was a paperback entitled *Myths and Folklore of the South West.*

That clinched it! It must be Roy's. Hastily Dayton flicked through the book and found several underlined passages and notations, all in pencil and instantly recognizable as Roy's handwriting. He found a section on Druidic practices and certain other primitive rites said to have been handed down from earlier periods. The name Arthur cropped up here and there, along with the usual references to Tintagel, then Dayton found a very brief passage on Penmire.

'. . . a very old settlement, believed to be the one-time centre of a very primitive culture, centred around the worship of the Sea . . . fantastic theory that the earliest inhabitants were settlers from the sinking of Atlantis . . . seems a rather fanciful notion . . . possibly the survivors from Lyonesse or counterpart . . .' Pencilled beside the passage was the word: DAGON?

'I'm closing now,' boomed a voice above him, and Dayton slammed the book shut with a start.

'Oh. Oh, really? I'll be off then. Always carry some light reading matter, you know.' He knows, Dayton thought. *What are these people hiding?* He forced a grin, reflecting that it was still relatively early.

'Keep on the road, sir. One step off and you're likely to sink for good into the marshes.'

Dayton rose, pocketing the book. 'Uh-huh. I expect it'll brighten up soon. Sorry to be a nuisance.' He left as casually as he could, stepping once more into the dank, oppressive mist. The stench of fish came even more strongly to his nostrils now. Still, he'd resigned himself to expect anything in this eerie place, even pixies. But he *was* being observed, he knew at once, and far more intensely than before. Then he saw the glowing, baleful eyes of the cats, never for a moment averting their gaze.

Dayton watched them as he started down the street, having decided to stop at the shop. To his horror he saw that there were now a number of dogs in the mist, all plodding along quietly, as though waiting the command to attack. This was fast becoming a nightmare. What had Roy meant by the pencilled 'Dagon'? Dayton recognized the name as that of a mythical sea-dwelling creature, though as far as he knew it had only appeared in fiction.

Faintly-defined houses slipped past as he hastily moved on, conscious now of several cats and dogs lurking at his heels, like a hungry pack. A flapping from above made him duck, to see a crow disappear into the gloom. Another house appeared ahead, but before he had taken another step he saw three pairs of eyes glowing in front of him.

What are they – wolves? He felt panic gripping him. They're trying to surround me! Dayton abruptly turned to his left and sprinted between the houses, anywhere to escape the lurking shadows. A bark behind him told him they were giving chase.

He came to the edge of the marsh, and for a moment he almost forgot the pursuit. He had found concrete proof that Roy had come to Penmire; one wheel and part of the front bumper of his Rover 2000 were sticking up out of the mire. Dayton had no time to speculate. Something heavy crashed into the back of his head and he plummeted into a bottomless well of oblivion.

Dayton came round with a splitting headache. His arms felt as though they were being torn from their sockets, and his mouth was horribly dry. Total darkness enveloped him; his surroundings swam in a blur as he tried to focus on something tangible. Vague thoughts on what had happened trickled back to him, but he was in no condition to struggle.

The first sound he heard was the plop-plop-plop of water somewhere near his head. He tried to move, only to find that he was chained up, back to a damp wall, somewhere in a cellar or cave. *Chained?* His mind raced as he tugged hopelessly in the chill, earthy air. There were scurrying sounds around his feet in response to his movements; he kicked out wildly, his toe digging into a number of squealing, furry bodies. The place was alive with rats, and as they ran hither and thither the air became permeated with the now familiar stink of rotting fish.

'Phil!' hissed a voice nearby, where more chains rattled in the acrid blackness.

'Roy? Is that you?' Dayton could not believe his ears.

''Fraid so, old pal. I was hoping you wouldn't get to find me.'

'What the devil's going on in this village? I've never encountered anything like it in all my travels.'

'I dread to think.' Baxter sounded very tired.

'The rudeness of the local goons I can stomach, but this is going too damn far.'

'Guess so. But save your strength, Phil. You'll probably need it.'

'I found a book of yours in the inn. I notice you've pencilled in a few notes. Have you any ideas on what's happening? Why the chains, for God's sake?' Rivulets of sweat trickled down Dayton's face despite the cold. His arms ached intolerably.

'Something very old and very evil has got Penmire in its grip, Phil. Whether they practise satanic rites or what, I don't know, but I've been shackled up here for bloody ages. I don't know for how long. I can't feel my arms. Some of the things I've heard . . . God, it's incredible!' Baxter gasped with the effort.

'Where exactly are we?'

'Under the chapel. You may have noticed it. Sort of crypt. Judging by some of the chanting that goes on up there – ' He broke off.

'What have you done for food? You must have been here for several days.'

'Oh, they keep me alive. Christ knows why, but they feed me. A robed figure in black appears now and again. It would be laughably melodramatic if it wasn't for the fact that I'm scared. Really scared, Phil. We're in a helluva situation.' Dayton admired his friend's strength of character; a lesser man would have cracked up in here. Even *he* might . . .

'It's insane,' he growled. 'I know about witchcraft and most of its various cults, but I can't believe these people would do us any serious harm. It must be some sort of hoax – a festival, do you think?' Dayton's nerves were rapidly fraying. He had to keep talking.

'The pain's real enough.'

'They'd never get away with it.'

'Oh no? What's to stop the police finding us in the mire? Or not finding us in the mire? No one is safe on these moors. It's one of the bleakest parts of England. We may as well be on Mars.'

'Cheerful bugger!' They were silent for a moment; the humour soon vanished.

'Well,' grunted Dayton at length, 'what do we do?'

'God knows. We can't break these chains. We just wait.'

So they waited, their minds uselessly trying to fathom a way to escape, but there was absolutely none. The seconds slipped into minutes, marked by the ever-dripping, wet walls, and the minutes turned slowly to hours. There was only the pain and discomfort as the scampering rats kept vigil over the two incarcerated men. At last they heard sounds above them – feet shuffling to and fro in the chapel. Dayton, who had slipped to his knees, cocked an ear. Faintly came the strains of weird, ethereal music, like fluted pipes, drifting out from the old walls into the night.

'Roy. Are you awake?' There was a grunt. 'What's that noise?'

'It's them again. It happens every now and then – nights, I suppose . . . Another . . . ritual.'

'You O.K.?'

'I'll do. You know that passage I marked in the book? Did

you see my reference to Dagon?'

'Yes, it's in my pocket.'

'Well, there could be something in it. It's a crazy notion, but now and again I've heard the name Dagon mentioned in the chanting. You listen for it once they start. One time I thought I heard something . . . out in the marsh. Like a huge wave breaking. Yes, I know it sounds bloody daft, but there was something.'

'Maybe not so daft, Roy. I came here across that marsh and some of the things I heard were pretty odd.'

'Such as?'

'People splashing about. And frogs. God, I never heard so many. All at once they started up in unison.'

They fell silent again. Baxter broke the lull with a forced snort.

'Humph! We're probably behaving like kids. I know we're in a right mess, but the moor *is* spooky. There are probably the usual scientific explanations for it all.'

'Perhaps. But I'd like a good explanation for this.' Dayton rattled his chains. 'I'll create bloody hell when I get back to civilization.'

'Quiet a sec!' They both listened anew to the strange noises from above. A deep, somehow obscene chanting had begun, the words totally indecipherable, utterly alien.

'There they go again. They'll go on for hours, working themselves up into a frenzy. Just when you think it'll die down, they start up again.'

'Again, this is all new to me. I wish I had a tape-recorder.'

'I'd settle for a wrench,' Baxter replied, but neither of them laughed.

All that night the blasphemous sound swelled until, in the early hours of the morning, it reached a peak. There were sounds from around the prisoners, sounds of slopping footsteps, though nothing could be seen in the dark; the fish odour was overpowering. The climax of the terrible dirge above came in a resounding thunderclap which shook the very foundations of the chapel. Its echoes rolled away into the distance.

'Roy, that sound! It's going away beneath us! I'm sure of it.'

'Eh?' Roy Baxter was exhausted, very drowsy, having only partly registered the boom. He couldn't take much more of this.

'Have you heard anything underground?' persisted Dayton.

'Underground? No. Only from up there,' Baxter said sleepily. Dayton was thinking of the marsh and the rippling motion that he had seen.

'Probably an echo,' Baxter suggested. 'There are lots of caves under the, er, village.'

'Caves?'

'Umm. Well, tunnels. I saw a few when they dragged me here. All man-made, though.'

'But what about the mire?' Caves running under that would be geologically impossible.

'I dunno. They seem to avoid that.' Baxter yawned. 'I expect they all go straight down.'

'Curious.' Somehow the two men lapsed into fitful sleep; time had ceased to exist for them in this rancid pit.

They languished for three days, three days of gruelling anguish which were broken only by the brief appearance of a robed, half-glimpsed figure who fed them. After that the villagers came for their prisoners. Above the cellar, the voices had begun chanting again in mournful unison. From out of the ether came whispered sounds of demonic laughter. Baxter and Dayton were too spent to complain as their chains were unlocked, and they were forced, staggering, through numerous cold puddles of muddy water, pushed along by the sinister robed figures of a score of unseen inhabitants.

They were led almost unconsciously along these subterranean, winding tunnels until they came out eventually into the open. Their bodies were weak and their spirits broken.

It was evening as they emerged; the sun was sinking into an orange sea of clouds, tinting the surrounding tors with gold. Wisps of glistening mist hung in shreds above the marsh, like steam rising from a sulphurous pool. The two men registered little of this. They were some distance from the village, at the edge of the marsh, and here they were thrust forward on to a huge, flat slab of granite. Thin beards of stubble darkened both their jaws, while their eyes were rimmed and bloodshot. Neither had the strength to look up at the diminishing glory of the sunset.

Roy Baxter began to mutter to himself, reciting the Lord's Prayer under his breath. Dayton's head lay against cold rock. He regarded his friend through pain-misted eyes; beside him the reeds trembled in the cool breeze.

'Roy. Roy!' he whispered hoarsely. The other turned to him, still praying. Above them the captors were still.

'We're done. Do you understand?'

'Listen!'

Far out over the marsh there came a gibbering of something nebulous, as though the mire itself were alive. The frogs had begun again that heart-stopping croaking – a hundred thousand throats swelling the chorus. Dayton turned his head, forcing a look back at the village, framed between the arms of two of the gaunt figures in black. There were scores of similarly-garbed people filing out of what he took to be the chapel, all with arms raised in supplication, all walking like jerky dolls towards the two outsiders and the marsh.

To whom or what are they praying? Dayton asked himself, unable to credit his eyes. With a start of revulsion he saw that there were a number of dogs, cats and even a few sheep staring placidly out at the marsh. The spell on Penmire gripped even the animals. The chant swelled and the words became clear, though still incomprehensible.

*'Ngah ohahgn, mnahn, ohahgn mnepn phatagn Dagon.*
*Ngah opahgan, rhantgna Dagon.*
*Ssna, ssna, phatagn Dagon.'*

Over and over they repeated it. These were words not written for human mouths to speak. I must get out now. God knows what they'll do, thought Dayton.

'Roy!' he whispered. 'Roy!' But his friend had passed out over the altar-like stone. Dayton feigned the same, one eye on the chanting crowd. Those around had taken up the chant as well. Bloody mumbo-jumbo.

All around the valley the sound of the frogs was growing in volume; louder and louder it came, blending malefically with the ululations of the oncoming worshippers. From the marshes came a rising cloud of dense vapour, and with it the unbearable fish-stench that Dayton had smelled so frequently. This time it seemed to pulse out from the marsh in disgusting waves, and he almost vomited.

Now he could see the frogs. They hopped around the stone as if mocking him – the marshes were teeming with them. Dayton shook himself. Beside him his captors were kneeling, arms outstretched in obeisance to the very heart of the marsh. What did they expect to see? Dayton craned his neck and gasped. Bubbles were bursting all over the surface as if it were boiling. He fought to control his sanity as he realized that th chanting was *attracting* something out in that festering poc of horror.

A movement beside him drew his attention back to hi immediate dilemma. He turned to see some of these devilis acolytes stretching Roy, still unconscious, over the altar stone preparing him for the very sacrifice he had feared. Dayto was stunned. *No, they can't mean it. Not today, 1974.* Bu they paid no attention to his torrent of invective. Dayto flung himself upon them with last reserves of energy, kicking biting, hammering with his fists. But it was useless. He wa flung contemptuously aside to roll pathetically into the reeds

Stark terror gripped him now. He got up, his movemen ignored by the still-chanting villagers, and fled into th treacherous mire, desperately trying to find a way through th numerous bogs. He looked back as he panted on, only to se a curved knife, glittering in the twilight with scarlet jewels raised high. This is madness, *madness*. Dayton averted his gaz and felt his stomach heave, refusing to believe the knife woul fall. But he heard it sink into Roy Baxter's flesh, and a shudder ing, satisfied sigh went up from the villagers.

*'Abaghna pnam pnam Dagon.*
*Accept our sacrifice, O Dagon.*
*Ssna ssna, phatagn Dagon.'*

Tears of disbelief coursed in grimy runnels down Dayton' face. He shook his head in utter disgust at what they had done Blood ran freely over the altar into the mud – Roy had die without a sound. Dayton fled farther into the marsh, hopin against hope to reach the tors before they came for him But further diabolic events were unfolding. From even th farthest reaches of the marsh the fish-smell was at its mo foul; a new element of horror was emerging.

Unspeakable shapes were thrusting up out of the oozing mu and green scum, shapes so dreadful, so appalling, that only i the wildest fantasies of a madman could they have bee conceived. Dayton bit into his hand to stifle a shriek. Th constant chanting was taking its effect, as had the spilling o blood, drawing these vile monstrosities up from the depths lik enchanted snakes. They were half-human, half-fish, or so looked, for their features were a repulsive blend of both, wit fins protruding from each jowl and long, plumed spin stretching right down their backs. There were gills in the man-like trunks, their eyes were the wide, filmy eyes of fish, and their arms were long and thin, tapering to webbed claws.

From these came the hellish smell. Dayton reached a boulder and leapt on to it, heart almost bursting with the effort. The mist was thickening, thankfully obscuring many of the beings, while the sun had set, leaving the world in rapidly-gathering darkness. Dayton was surrounded by the fish-men, who still continued to rise from the muck like a legion from hell itself. As he stared in fascination, they began emitting croaking sounds of their own, frog-like and deep, until with a shudder Dayton realized that they were chanting in response to the people of Penmire.

From thick, fleshy lips came the same dread words that the villagers were chanting, spoken, he saw, by the very ones *to whom the language belonged.* Although he was some way out in the marsh, none of the terrible people came near. They just waved and writhed gently from side to side as though drugged, arms raised in ecstasy as were those of the villagers. Frogs jumped everywhere, their croaks adding to the swelling din.

Dayton ached with weariness; there was not a muscle in his body that didn't crave rest, but he knew that he must keep on whilst the horde were preoccupied with their incantations. He sprang from the rock and zigzagged his faltering way through islands of turf, constantly sinking to his knees into clinging mud. He wanted to lie down and sleep, but dare not. The thought of that dripping knife gave him more will to go on. Still the creatures were ignoring him, though he passed within feet of several, shutting everything out of his mind except the tors and escape.

Suddenly the ground heaved, pitching him forward into the gurgling slime, so that for terrifying seconds he crawled with cold, reptilian frogs. Within moments he was knee-deep, jerking himself upright and yanking at his arms to get them free. They came out with great sucking sounds, but his feet were held. He beat frantically at the swarming frogs, feeling them squirming beneath him in multitudes. Dayton struggled in despair. He was trapped. And still the chanting went on, rising in volume, driving him ever-closer to madness. Now the ground began rippling and pulsing like a great heart beating. A note of joy had entered the chanting.

Dayton heard, *felt,* the sound from below. He could not put a name to it, nor dared to do so. Excitement spurred the invocations around him, and he tried to twist and see what exactly the villagers were doing: were they pursuing, or had they forgotten him in the midst of their insane revels? But he could not see. He was stuck firmly, sinking inexorably to a gruesome death.

*'Ngah ohahgn, phatagn Dagon.*
*Abaghna pnam pnan hnam Dagon.*
*Accept our second sacrifice, O Dagon.*
*Ssna ssna, phatagn Dagon.'*

Dayton heard the words of the people behind, and the terrible implication. He had escaped the knife, but the mire would take him. Unless . . . With a last, vain effort, he stripped off his jacket, ready to throw it in front of him in one final attempt to heave himself out. Then he stopped, eyes wide in utter disbelief. Before him the marsh was heaving and thrashing like the cauldron of a volcano, sending great plumes of mud high into the mist. Dayton felt more tremors in the rumbling ground.

The chanting had abruptly ceased, together with the croaking of the frogs, as all eyes, all arms, had turned to the source of the disturbance. From out of the unknown depths of the mire, ringed by the evil-smelling fish-creatures, something huge, something unutterably ancient was rising. Dayton screamed now, his whole body shaking uncontrollably, unable to free itself from the fatal clutches of the marsh.

Higher and higher rose the mire-coated colossus, and worse grew the unholy stench of that awesome thing. For this was Dagon, Dagon the ageless, summoned at last from an eternal sleep, summoned from the refuge he had sought untold aeons before, when he and all his kind were cursed upon earth.

Up, up rose the towering horror, a throbbing, glistening mass of scaley, amorphous life. Waves of mud, spilling over with frogs, rippled out from the growing monster. A score of thick, oily, tentacle-like protruberances, coated in contracting suckers, whipped up from beneath the ooze in a welter of steaming filth, as the titanic creature rose higher, exuding an aura of clinging vapours. Dayton coughed as he caught the first whiffs of the poisonous diffusion; he had sunk waist deep before it, his eyes riveted on this thing from before the dawn of men.

All around in the night the servants bowed down, eager to serve, smiting themselves and yelling out in exultation. Dagon of the deeps had come. Come to begin a new reign. The earth shook constantly, hissing with escaping steam, and the mire overspilled its contaminated ooze out into the village. Dayton closed his eyes and prayed fervently, sinking lower, lower. Dagon stretched out his many arms to receive the sacrifice that his people had prepared.

# ACKNOWLEDGEMENTS

The Editor gratefully acknowledges permission to use copyright material to the following:

Kay Leith for *For The Love of Pamela*. © Kay Leith 1974

Sydney J. Bounds for *The Mask* and *Hothouse*. Both © Sydney J. Bounds 1974

Joyce Marsh for *Old Hether's Picture*. © Joyce Marsh 1974

Bernard Taylor and Michael Bakewell & Associates Ltd. for *Cera* and *My Very Good Friend*. Both © Bernard Taylor 1974

Pamela Vincent for *Lost Soul* and *Homicidal Maniac!* Both © Pamela Vincent 1974

A. E. Ellis for *If Thy Right Hand offend Thee...* © A. E. Ellis 1974

Martin Ricketts for *Dissolving Partnership* and *And Now The Pact*. Both © Martin Ricketts 1974

Terry Gisbourne for *The Quiet Man*. © Terry Gisbourne 1974

Frances Stephens and Michael Bakewell & Associates Ltd. for *A Walk Along The Beach*. © Frances Stephens 1974

R. Chetwynd-Hayes for *The Catomado*. © R. Chetwynd-Hayes 1974

Dorothy K. Haynes for *Dorothy Dean*. © Dorothy K. Haynes 1974

Julia Birley for *The Old Men*. © Julia Birley 1974

Adrian Cole for *The Horror Under Penmire*. © Adrian Cole 1974

Every effort has been made to trace the owners of the copyright material in this book. In the case of any question arising as to the use of any material, the editor would be pleased to receive notification of this.